DENE OF THE SECRET SERVICE

Bound for Liverpool to board his Japanese ship, *Oki Maru*, a Korean seaman is murdered and his identity assumed by his killer. Then, after the ship sails, it disappears — presumed lost in a storm . . . The owner of a remote country house in Wales is pressured into selling it — then brutally murdered. Meanwhile, when secret documents relating to a draft treaty with Japan go missing from the Foreign Office, agent Dene of the Secret Service has orders to recover them . . .

Books by Gerald Verner
in the Linford Mystery Library:

THE LAST WARNING

GERALD VERNER

DENE OF THE SECRET SERVICE

Complete and Unabridged

LINFORD
Leicester

First published in Great Britain

First Linford Edition
published 2011

British Library CIP Data

Verner, Gerald.
   Dene of the Secret Service. - -
(Linford mystery library)
1. Intelligence officers- -Great Britain- -
Fiction. 2. Sailors- -Crimes against- -Fiction.
3. Identity theft- -Fiction. 4. Homeowners
- -Crimes against- -Wales- -Fiction.
5. Great Britain. Foreign Office- -Fiction.
6. Detective and mystery stories.
7. Large type books.
I. Title II. Series
823.9'12–dc22

ISBN 978–1–44480–649–6

Published by
F. A. Thorpe (Publishing)
Anstey, Leicestershire

Set by Words & Graphics Ltd.
Anstey, Leicestershire
Printed and bound in Great Britain by
T. J. International Ltd., Padstow, Cornwall

1

The Mate of the 'Oki Maru'

That death was very close to him — death, watchful and soft-footed — K'Yung had no idea, as he settled himself in a corner seat of the long midnight express that was to bear him from the fog-bound London terminus to the distant docks of Liverpool. But death had followed K'Yung for many hours that night.

The average Londoner would have taken K'Yung either for a Japanese or for a citizen of the vast ramshackle Chinese Republic. But K'Yung was neither. He was a Korean.

With thin, parchment-coloured fingers, he took from the pocket of his badly-fitting, German-made suit a packet of cigarettes, lit one, peering out through the window into the misty gloom of the vast, echoing terminus.

He was alone in the compartment. He

was still alone when, in answer to the scream of the guard's whistle, the big express began slowly to draw out on its long journey through the night.

For a while the Korean watched the confused medley of signal lights — red, green, and yellow — floating past in the murk.

After a time he was disturbed by the arrival of a ticket-inspector; the official slid the door of the compartment shut on leaving, and vanished along the corridor. K'Yung bent down and drew out from beneath his seat the battered suitcase — purchased years before in Yokohama — that contained most of his worldly possessions. From it he took a creased English newspaper, and settled back in his corner to read — a somewhat laborious business, for though he could speak English fairly well, reading it was always a difficulty; wherefore he lost no chance of practice. For English is the international language among men of the sea, and the sea was K'Yung's profession in life.

He had arrived in London some

2

months before as second mate of a Japanese tramp-steamer, the *Funakawa Maru*. While the ship had been lying in the West India Docks, K'Yung had contracted blood-poisoning in one arm, and had been in hospital when the *Funakawa Maru* had sailed from London. Now, with his arm well again, he was being hurried to Liverpool by the shipping agents to join another of the same company's vessels, the *Oki Maru*. All Japanese boats are surnamed Maru; in Japanese the word means 'ship.'

The *Oki Maru* was to sail on the following day, with K'Yung signed on as second mate in place of a man who had been swept overboard in the Irish Sea. She was bound for Cho-Sen, Korea, and K'Yung, who had not seen his native land for five years, was well pleased in consequence with his appointment to the *Oki Maru*.

Flattening the day-old newspaper on his knees, the wiry little Korean began to spell out to himself, letter by letter, the first headline that caught his eyes.

'FOREIGN OFFICE SENSATION'

What the Foreign Office was, K'Yung had no idea at all. But he persevered with the paragraph beneath, as the long express, with smooth-rushing wheels, raced on through the gloom along the gleaming ribbons of steel.

'Whether or not there is any foundation for the insistent rumour that certain secret papers have recently been found to be missing from the Foreign Office, the public cannot know for certain, since Whitehall declines to issue any statement. But it is undoubtedly believed in several responsible quarters that a draft copy of the proposed treaty with the Japanese Government concerning trade rights in Korea has been stolen, presumably through the machinations of foreign agents in London, and if this is indeed the case, the country has a right to know who is responsible for the laxity which could render possible so grave an occurrence. So the gentlemen of Whitehall really treat their duties to the nation so lightly that — '

K'Yung laid the paper down. It had taken him a long time to read so far, and a great deal of the paragraph had been quite incomprehensible to him. Interested though he had been to find a reference to Korea, the labour of reading more did not appeal to him just then. He lit another cigarette, and turned his attention to the window. Pulling the blind aside for a moment he peered out.

The express was in lonely country now. The echoing roar of the train filled the compartment, flung back from the high, rocky walls of a deep cutting through which it was racing, the billowing smoke-clouds from the giant locomotive beating down against the windows in ghostly fashion. K'Yung's eyes closed.

The roar of the speeding train beat insistently in his ears, grew vaguer, until finally all sounds were lost to him as he sank into the easy sleep of the Oriental.

He was still sleeping when a noiseless shadow appeared in the corridor outside his compartment. Two jet-black eyes stared in at him, set in a yellow-brown face. A moment or two later, lean hands were softly drawing the door of the compartment sideways.

Noiseless as a cat, the newcomer stepped into the compartment, and slid the door shut behind him.

Calmly, without hurry, the intruder drew down the blinds of the windows overlooking the corridor. Turning again, he stood surveying the sleeping, huddled figure of K'Yung in the far corner. He spoke softly — as if to satisfy himself that the other man really slept. Had K'Yung heard, he would have recognised the tongue as that of Korea, though the intruder was dressed, like himself, in western clothes. Nor had he spent all his life in Korea. He was very well known in certain circles of Tokio.

Very quietly the vision crossed the compartment. He stood above the sleeping man, staring down at K'Yung with a snaky glitter in his narrow eyes.

There was a sudden dull clap of sound as the train plunged into a tunnel-mouth. The abrupt change in the sound of the train caused the second mate of the *Oki Maru* to open his eyes and lift his head. A flash of surprise leapt into his face as he became aware of the figure standing there. And then strong fingers had him by the throat, and before he had time even to wonder what the motive for this attack could be, he found himself fighting fiercely, all the cards against him, already half-strangled as he was by that lean hand fastened relentlessly upon his throat.

The attacker was the bigger man of the two, even though not tall by English standards. But K'Yung was a fighter, and the look in those merciless, snake-like eyes that glittered down into his own told him that he was fighting for his life.

Something appeared in the attacker's free hand — a small rubber truncheon drawn from beneath his coat, heavy enough, small though it was, to beat out a man's brains. K'Yung, writhing in his corner, pinned down against the cushions by the steely yellow hand at his throat, saw the truncheon whip upwards. With a supreme effort, he drove home a foot in his antagonist's stomach, and the hand at which his own fingers clawed relaxed as the other staggered back with an agonised grunt.

K'Yung drew in a whistling breath between his open teeth, filling his aching lungs with the air for which they had fought. In a flash he was on his feet. The truncheon came swinging for his head.

Had K'Yung been at all familiar with English trains he could have reached the communication-cord. But he knew nothing of such things, and the other man was between him and the door to the corridor. As the truncheon fell he twisted aside, and felt a dull, agonising blow on the shoulder in the same moment that he hurled himself at his attacker.

There was a knife in K'Yung's hand now, an ugly little weapon with a short, curved blade, snatched from the belt beneath his waistcoat. But a hand closed round his wrist, forcing the knife upwards above his head. With straining arms, reeling to the sway of the rushing train, the two men interlocked.

The express had emerged once more into open country. Beyond the drawn blinds a dark and lonely countryside lay stretched, without a light to break the dim expanse of shadowy woods and fields. With a hollow rush they passed over a river bridge, and together they were flung in a struggling heap against the carriage door as the train swept round a banked curve, on the crest of a high embankment. Dazed and panting, K'Yung lay sprawled with his head against the carriage seat, his knife fallen from his fingers, his left hand clawed on the other's face as he gouged desperately at his antagonist's eyes. Then something crashed down upon his skull.

His brain seemed to be on fire. Dancing, flickering lights swam before his eyes, and a strange mist seemed suddenly to have filled the compartment. Out of the mist the face of the unknown Korean glared down at him — black eyes set in a yellow-brown skin, a long scratch down one cheek, from which blood was oozing in tiny drops and smears.

K'Yung stirred feebly. Then once more the rubber truncheon beat down upon his head, and he sank back, limp. Again and again, and there was blood upon the rubber.

K'Yung lay very still.

The killer rose unsteadily to his feet, balancing himself against the swaying of the narrow compartment. He stood staring down at the dead body of K'Yung with impassive face, wiping the blood from the long scratch on his own cheek. A murmur of satisfaction stirred his lips, then abruptly he glanced swiftly behind him towards the door.

Someone was coming along the corridor outside.

Quickly the murderer bent down and thrust the body out of sight under one of the seats. But the precaution proved unnecessary. The footsteps in the corridor passed on and died away, lost in the echoing clatter of the train.

The killer drew his victim out into view again, running swiftly over the dead man's pockets, transferring their contents to his own. A swift examination of K'Yung's suitcase proved satisfactory. The murderer was in possession of his victim's uniform and papers — everything necessary to prove his identity, apparently, at least, as the second mate of the *Oki*

Maru. There would be no reason in the world next morning for the Japanese skipper to suspect for a moment that the Korean who arrived at the ship to take up the job of second mate, preparatory to the *Oki Maru*'s long voyage to the Yellow Sea, was not the man he had been told to expect, but an impostor in a dead man's place.

The killer raised the blind that covered the window of the carriage door and lowered the glass sash. He peered out into the rushing darkness.

Far away, a single signal light was burning in the vast expanse of lonely country that stretched between the railway line and the distant dark horizon. It vanished as a belt of black wood came sweeping past. Thrusting out his head, the man from Tokio peered along the train in either direction.

Turning, he dragged the limp form of the dead man against the carriage door. His fingers went to the handle, thrusting the door open, and the huddled shape fell half out on to the wind-swept footboard. The murderer bent down and swung the dead thing out into the night, and the tearing wind crashed the door shut.

There was blood upon the floor. The man from Tokio took up the dead man's newspaper and wiped it up carefully, tossing the hideously-stained sheets out through the open window. The rubber truncheon, after a moment or two of doubt, followed, and the killer closed the window with a thin smile, and drew the blind.

Calmly he lit one of the dead man's cigarettes, and dropped into the corner seat.

With racing wheels, the long, darkened express thundered on through the night, towards the distant north-west coast, bearing the man from Tokio nearer with every flying second to the ship bound for the Yellow Sea.

★   ★   ★

Black-hulled, with a green band just below her scupper edge, grey-funnelled, her owner's colours encircling the grey in two wide stripes, the *Oki Maru* was a second-hand English steamer of four thousand odd tons. She had passed into

Japanese ownership some six years before. That the Korean who had arrived that morning from London to take up the duties of second mate was anything other than the man he appeared to be, the little Japanese skipper had no reason to doubt, as, with her red-and-white flag floating at her stern, the *Oki Maru* headed down the Mersey and steamed away into the setting sun. She met the great grey waves and turned south, with the weather-glass in the chart-room falling with a sinister rapidity.

The storm hit her about midnight.

At three o'clock in the morning — six bells of the second mate's watch — an SOS from the *Oki Maru* was picked up by various ships. At that hour the storm was at its height — an inferno of shrieking wind and foaming seas beneath a pitch-black sky, out of which the voice of the Japanese steamer was heard once, like the despairing prayer of a dying man; once, but no more. No bearings were given. The message had snapped off unfinished.

With the dawn the gale slackened. But of the *Oki Maru* nothing was heard or seen.

She had vanished — without trace.

13

2

Two Mysteries

Trevor Lowe glanced up from the deep chair in which he was seated as Arnold White came in. His secretary had been to the post office.

'What do you make of this, White?'

Lowe rose to his feet with the abrupt question, taking the pipe from his lips, an expression of frowning thought on his face as he held out an opened letter, written on expensive grey notepaper. White took it with a questioning glance and read the signature.

'Letitia Delmar?' he asked aloud. 'I seem to know the name.'

'You've met her,' nodded Lowe. 'She is the niece of Sir Matthew Moncrieff, you remember. Old friend of mine. He has an old place in Wales, and his niece lives with him.'

Arnold nodded. He remembered now.

'Dear Mr. Lowe, — Could you possibly come to Trecallyn immediately? I cannot explain why in a letter, but I am so terribly frightened. I don't know what it's all about. My uncle refused to trouble you, but if you could possibly come — at once — I should be terribly grateful.

'LETITIA DELMAR.'

The secretary handed the letter back. 'Queer,' he remarked.

'The question is, is this caused by some imaginative fancy on the part of a young girl living in a lonely house? Or is there good cause for it? We can't afford the time to trek into the wilds of Wales on a fool's errand. And the fact that old Moncrieff himself, as she admits, declines to refer the matter — whatever it is — to me, rather points to the fact that it is not so serious as his niece imagines.'

'From what I remember of her, she seemed a fairly level-headed sort of a girl,' commented White thoughtfully. 'But we are a bit busy just now, as you say.'

Lowe tapped the stem of his pipe

15

against his teeth, frowning. Through the open window the sounds of the traffic in Portland Place came murmuring to their ears.

'Still — an old friend, White. Perhaps it would be better if we went, if only to calm Miss Delmar's fears, whatever they may be. If it is a fool's errand, we can be back in London tomorrow. And if not, we shall be glad we went.'

'Then you intend to go?'

'Yes.' Lowe's voice was incisive — he had made up his mind. 'I have to look in at the Yard this morning; Shadgold is anxious to see me about something. After I've seen him we can set off for Wales. We'll go by car.'

Detective-inspector Shadgold, of Scotland Yard, was never backward in asking advice and help from the dramatist, even though he was inclined at times to be a trifle galled by the successes Lowe usually made. The bull-dog jawed inspector greeted his friend with a warm hand-clasp when, some little time later, Lowe entered the small office overlooking the Thames Embankment in New Scotland Yard.

16

'Good of you to look in, Mr. Lowe.'

'I'm just off to Wales, Shadgold.' Lowe dropped into a chair and took out his pipe. 'Hurry-call from a very charming young acquaintance of mine. So if you can be brief — '

'Sure I'll be brief,' growled Shadgold. 'Baccy?' He had produced his pouch. 'Like your own better, eh? Listen, Lowe, you remember that case of the dead Korean who was found about a month ago lying smashed up on a railway embankment near Wynford?'

Lowe nodded.

'I remember. It's believed he was murdered by another Korean, named K'Yung, in the night express to Liverpool. A ticket inspector remembered seeing two yellow men on the train in different compartments. K'Yung sailed as second mate on board the *Oki Maru*, which is presumed to have gone down in that big storm the ship ran into soon after leaving Liverpool. A rubber truncheon was found farther along the line, which K'Yung is supposed to have murdered his man with, and thrown out of the train after chucking

17

the body out. The victim had been hit by another train, and was badly mangled. He was never identified.'

'You always have everything at your fingertips, don't you?' grunted Shadgold.

'That's my hobby,' smiled Lowe. 'Well, what about it? Whoever the dead Korean was, and whatever the motive behind the murder, fate stepped in, apparently, and did the hangman's job for him when the murderer went down with the *Oki Maru*!'

'It looked like it,' answered Shadgold slowly. 'But — suppose the *Oki Maru* did not go down in that storm? Suppose she didn't — and that K'Yung, the murderer of that unidentified man found by the railway line, is still alive and kicking?'

Lowe glanced at him sharply. A note of blank triumph had crept into Shadgold's voice.

'What do you mean?'

'You remember — since you remember everything — that no trace of the *Oki Maru* was ever found,' went on Shadgold. 'That was queer in those waters. Not a lifebelt, not a floating grating — nothing!'

'Yes, that was queer,' assented the

dramatist. 'Well?'

'If you ask me, there's a big mystery behind the disappearance of that Japanese tramp. And if her second mate, the Korean, K'Yung, is still alive, the Yard wants him.'

'Naturally. But what on earth do you imagine happened to the *Oki Maru* if she did not go down for good in that storm? And why should you believe for a moment that the Korean can still be alive?'

'What happened to the *Oki Maru* is a big mystery,' repeated Shadgold. 'As for the Korean — ' He broke off, and crossed to his desk, picking up a memoranda-pad. 'There's a firm in Birkenhead, Mr. Lowe, named White & Collins, who deal, among other things, in ships' chronometers. Some days ago a man whom they took to be a Chinese sold them a ship's chronometer — an almost new one, in good condition. They gave him eighteen pounds for it. One of the firm's employees, however, suspected the man — didn't think him quite straight. It was just instinct. Inquiries were made, and the chronometer was identified as that of the *Oki Maru*.'

Shadgold grinned complacently at the look of astonishment that had appeared on Lowe's face.

'That's puzzled you? If the *Oki Maru* went down in that storm, how did her chronometer come to be sold in Birkenhead in perfectly good condition not long afterwards?'

'Anything more?' Lowe leaned forward in his chair.

'Yes. Fingerprints on the chronometer were found to be identical with those on the truncheon with which K'Yung, the *Oki Maru's* second mate, is believed to have murdered his unidentified victim. The supposed Chinese who sold that chronometer was the second mate, the Korean — alive and kicking.'

The dramatist drew slowly and thoughtfully at his pipe. He was interested in the riddle that Shadgold had put before him, as his whole expression showed.

'What do you make of it, Mr. Lowe?'

'Nothing — at present. It is rather bewildering. The *Oki Maru* sent out a broken SOS that night, didn't she? And nothing more was heard or seen of her. But if she had gone down in the storm it's a physical impossibility for her chronometer to have turned up in good condition only a few days ago. Therefore, she did not go down in the storm. But what actually happened to her — '

He broke off with a frown, and Shadgold chuckled. It was not very often that he had the pleasure of so completely bewildering his friend.

'I suppose they've tried to trace the Korean?' added Lowe.

The other nodded.

'Yes, but without any success. After leaving White & Collins' place his movements are quite unknown. That's why I asked you to look in. I thought it was a pretty enough little problem to interest you a good deal. Interesting enough, perhaps, for you to like to lend a hand at finding this murderer, K'Yung. Whether or not that murder of his has anything to do with the mystery of the *Oki Maru* — '

'Sorry, but I'm afraid I'm too busy just

now to lend you a hand in the affair,' cut in Lowe, rather regretfully. He glanced at his watch, and rose to his feet. 'In fact, I must be getting along. White's waiting outside with the car — I told you we're off to Wales? I should be very interested to hear any developments, though, regarding the Korean mate and the *Oki Maru*. What line are you working on?'

Shadgold looked a little disconcerted.

'Well, as a matter of fact, I haven't a line at all,' he confessed shortly. 'There seems no starting-off point to pick up the man's trail — or the ship's. I was hoping you might hit on some way of tackling the problem.'

Lowe smiled. The truth was out — it had not been so much that Shadgold had wished to put him on to a peculiarly interesting case as that, completely baffled by the mystery of it, he had hoped to pick his friend's brains for its elucidation.

Lowe shook his head smilingly.

'Sorry, old man. Can't see my way to lending a hand. Not just now, anyway. Later on, when I am a bit more free, if you're still flummoxed as to how to get your man — the Korean — maybe I'll see what I can do. Let me know.' Again he smiled at Shadgold's disappointed face. 'I'll admit I'm sorry not to be more helpful. The problem of this missing Jap steamer and her mysterious second officer intrigues me considerably. By the way, what do Lloyd's say about it?'

'The insurance on the *Oki Maru* is being held up, of course.'

'Can't blame 'em for that,' said Lowe. 'And of course they are anxious for the mystery to be solved?'

'Yes,' growled Shadgold ill-humouredly. 'Though how in blazes — '

'Easier said than done, eh?' chuckled Lowe. 'Well, I wish you luck, Shadgold. And, as I say, let me know any developments.'

'I will,' nodded Shadgold. Lowe turned towards the door, and the Yard man moved towards it with him. 'Met a pal of yours this morning, by the way — Michael Dene.'

'Dene?' Lowe glanced at Shadgold in surprise. 'I thought he was abroad?'

Michael Dene, of the British Intelligence Service, which is more popularly known to the 'man in the street' as the Secret Service, was an old friend of Lowe's, though for long periods they never met, for Dene was a constant globetrotter, equally at home in London, Paris, or Amsterdam, New York, Belgrade, or Bucharest, or any other of the world's capitals. He came and went mysteriously, unknown and unperceived, a relentless worker for 'the Department' — the Intelligence Department of the Foreign Office. 'No. 55' — his official soubriquet in the Department — was a law unto himself.

'Just back from somewhere or other,' explained Shadgold. 'Happened to run into him in the Strand. Like me, he's interested in things Japanese at the moment.'

'What do you mean?'

'I believe he's come home to work on that business of the stolen draft of the Japanese treaty. You remember about that, of course. The Press got hold of the story. There's been the deuce of a row, though

24

it doesn't seem to have been anyone's fault. It's a mystery who stole the treaty draft, and how. Dene's on the job now, I'm pretty certain.'

'That's interesting,' said Lowe. 'Queer devil, Dene.'

White was as interested as Lowe had been to learn of the unexpected presence of Dene in London. But, like Lowe, he realised that in all probability they would see nothing of him during his presence in England; the next they heard of him would probably be to learn that he was far away once more from Whitehall, in Sofia, or Buenos Aires, or some such distant spot. Michael Dene usually counted miles in thousands.

Threading through the traffic, heading for the Great West Road — with Wales beyond — Lowe told his secretary of the problem that Shadgold had placed before him, the strange mystery of the *Oki Maru* and its murderous second mate. The riddle of the lost ship was entirely baffling; and yet obviously there was no possible answer to the question regarding the fate of the lost Japanese steamer.

'Suppose she rode the storm all night, but her radio was put out of action, and couldn't be repaired?' suggested White. 'If they just kept on, out into the Atlantic, and didn't happen to meet any other ships, to recognise them — '

'Then how could her chronometer have turned up in Birkenhead? A ship can't be navigated without a chronometer, in any case, roughly speaking. No, that won't explain it, Shadgold is right; there is some big mystery behind the disappearance of the *Oki Maru*. And if Shadgold can't clear it up, I shall tackle it myself later on!'

They were passing along the Mall. By the Palace, Lowe turned the big car into Constitution Hill, and they sped up the tree-lined gradient towards Hyde Park Corner.

'Meanwhile,' he added with a dry smile, 'we find out what — if anything — lies behind Miss Delmar's SOS from Wales!'

That their present quest could be leading them, in its own strange fashion, directly to the heart of the mystery of the

Oki Maru, was the very last thought in the minds of either, as the long grey Rolls raced westwards to pick up the road to Wales and the lonely old house where lived Sir Matthew Moncrieff and his lovely niece — the girl whose puzzling call had started them upon their journey.

3

The House in Wales

Sir Matthew Moncrieff, a fragrant Corona between his lips, stood listening to the stormy wind that was buffeting the great window at the end of the long room. A man of sixty odd, spare of build, with a pair of penetrating blue eyes and iron-grey hair, upright as a bayonet; a skin that showed him to be a man who had spent a considerable portion of his life east of the Suez; lean but powerful hands that told of a strength that was more than merely physical — Matthew Moncrieff, late of the Diplomatic Service, well-known authority on obscure Asiatic languages, made a striking figure, in the firelight of the big room, with his shadow flung in fantastic form on the opposite wall.

Night was closing in round the big house. But through the windows the wild outlines of the mountains could still be seen sharply defined against the darkening sky.

Hands clasped behind his back, Moncrieff stood motionless, staring with shadowed eyes at the opposite wall. From the tip of his cigar a thin wisp of grey smoke trailed — the ash had just fallen unheeded to the carpet. There was a frown on the handsome face of the solitary figure in the big, firelit room.

He had known this big house that stood in the shadow of the Welsh mountains, within a quarter mile of the great cliffs against which the Atlantic breakers foamed and thundered, since his boyhood days. But that day he had taken a step that was to sever his connection with the lonely old place for all time. The shadow in his eyes spoke of his regret — though not of remorse. When Matthew Moncrieff made a decision, it was final.

He did not notice the deepening darkness closing in upon him; did not hear the gusty beating of the wind against the great window-panes. His thoughts alone gripped him, to the exclusion of all else — until a sudden soft movement by the door, and the unexpected blaze of electric light around him as the lamps were switched on, caused him to glance quickly towards the door.

A girl was standing in the doorway.

'Hallo, Letitia!'

Letitia Delmar, Moncrieff's niece and ward, closed the door and crossed the room towards him. She was a girl in the early twenties, dark-haired and graceful, her face pale but very lovely in the soft lamp-light, with its delicately-moulded lips and shapely forehead. Moncrieff took the cigar from his lips and forced a smile. 'Good news for you, my dear!'

'You — you mean — ' Her voice faltered eagerly.

He took her hand, patting it.

'Yes,' he answered gravely. 'I have accepted that offer. I am selling the house. I signed the agreement of sale today. You realise what this means? Madame D'Elange stipulated for instant occupation. She takes over the house tomorrow — lock, stock, and barrel! Rather curious, her insistence on such immediate occupation; but considering the price she has offered, it would have been foolish to question her whims, eh, my dear?'

The pale face of Letitia Delmar lighted up strangely.

'You — you are doing this for me?' she whispered breathlessly.

He nodded.

'Yes. I've come to the conclusion that I've been a bit selfish, keeping you here in this lonely, out-of-the-world spot, at your age. All very well for me — I've known this house so long. Naturally, I — I love it. I'll admit it hurts a bit, leaving it. But you are young. It means nothing to you. And it is not fair to keep you a prisoner here in the wilds any longer. I see that now. Tomorrow we leave for London. The servants will follow as soon as we have found a house. Chambers, the agents, are going to look out for something we'll like. Till then, it'll mean an hotel.'

The girl's dark eyes were alight and eager. Then her quick smile died.

'You'll hate going,' she said slowly.

31

Again he shrugged.

'I'll get over it! Although I've known the place so long, it's not as if I have lived here for much of my life. Only a few years since I came back from Singapore, after all! The fact that I lived here as a youngster isn't going to make me force you to waste your youth and beauty among these mountains! London, social life, gaiety — that's what you need, and by James, you're going to have it.'

He smiled down at her.

'Only fair, my dear!'

'It's — wonderful of you,' she said quietly. Her eyes went to the uncurtained windows. Beyond, the mighty outlines of the mountains rose dark and ominous, almost sinister in the deepening gloom; and suddenly she shivered. 'I shall be glad to get away — yes. I'm only sorry that it means a sacrifice for you. But I'm frightened. You know why — '

'Nonsense, my dear! Imagination! Still, we are going, so — '

'Imagination!' she broke in quickly. 'No! Is it my imagination that queer people have been coming here at night, creeping round the house in the darkness? Is it my imagination that the two dogs have been found dead in the plantation?' She caught her breath with a little shudder. 'And that night I thought I saw someone actually in the house, in the long gallery — '

She broke off sharply, casting a quick glance at the window, and drew closer to her uncle. Moncrieff patted her shoulder, and crossed to the window, drawing the curtains across.

'There have been gypsies in the neighbourhood, we know,' he said gruffly. 'You can take it from me that it was they who came sneaking round here once or twice, seeing if there was anything to be picked up. As for the dogs, they must have picked up something poisonous in the grounds. The night you thought you saw someone in the long gallery — '

'Well?' she asked, half defiantly, as he broke off.

'That, I am convinced, was imagination, my dear. Your nerves had been upset, and you thought you saw someone. Not difficult, when one's nerves are wrong. We searched the house, and there was no one except ourselves and the servants! But it simply shows it's not good for you to stay any longer in this lonely place. The sooner we get away the better. And with this French lady offering us an excellent price just at this time — '

'I hope Madame D'Elange won't lose her nerve, too, after she has been here a little while!' the girl interrupted with a little unsteady smile. 'You've been a dear, to sell the house — because of me. It makes me wonder if I have been absurd, imagining things, as you say. And I have a confession to make.'

'A confession?'

'Yes, I didn't know you were going to sell the house, and I wrote to Mr. Lowe. I asked him to come here! I — I thought perhaps he — '

'The deuce, you did!' Moncrieff smiled dryly. 'Well, it will be very pleasant to see Lowe again, if he comes. I haven't seen him for a year or two — not since that time we ran into him during a visit to London. Hope he comes.'

'But when I suggested asking him to

come, you said no!'

'Didn't want to bring him here on a wild-goose chase, Letitia. He's a busy man. But since you have written to him of your own accord — '

'He might be here at any time, if he got my letter this morning. I — I didn't like to tell you. But if he does turn up, of course, he'll have to stay the night. I've told Hurst to have a room ready.'

'Well, that's good,' agreed Sir Matthew dryly. 'Any more news?'

She laughed.

'No, that's all! Why — listen — '

Above the noise of the wind beating round the old house, the hum of a car's engine had come abruptly to their ears. Letitia Delmar ran to the window and drew back one of the curtains. The dim glow of twin headlamps could be seen approaching the house down the long, oak-lined drive. The light of them hit the window as the nearing car curved into the wide, stone-flagged courtyard before the house, and the girl let the curtain fall back into place, turning eagerly to her uncle.

'It must be Mr. Lowe!'

'Well, he is your guest, my dear! Better go and welcome him,' suggested Moncrieff smilingly.

Letitia Delmar hurried from the room, and across the big stone-floored, vaulted hall to the great door at the far side. A manservant, who had evidently heard the car also, had appeared, through the door that led from the servants' quarters.

'All right, Hurst!'

The manservant withdrew, and the girl opened the door herself and went quickly out on to the steps. Two figures were alighting from the stationary car, drawn up outside.

'Mr. Lowe?' she called eagerly.

'At your service!' came the answer in pleasant tones; and the tall figure of Trevor Lowe appeared in the range of light, mounting the steps with White at his heels.

'So you've come!' she breathed. 'How good of you! Of course, you can stay the night?' she added, as they shook hands.

'If we shan't be in the way,' answered Lowe, smiling. 'Otherwise, we can easily put up at the nearest village. I take it Sir Matthew is not exactly expecting us, judging from your letter?'

'Oh, I've just told him you might come!' she laughed. 'He's looking forward to seeing you. But he thinks I have wasted your time by bringing you here on a wild-goose chase. Now you are here I am beginning to feel afraid I may have done. But it is so good of you to have come! I — I'll explain everything in a minute.'

She had stepped back into the hall. Lowe followed her, but White remained on the steps.

'Can I put the car away somewhere, Miss Delmar?' he asked.

'Oh, yes, of course. I'll show you the way round to the garage. Let me take you to my uncle first, Mr. Lowe. He's in the library.'

'Don't bother, Miss Delmar. I'll find him. I've been in this house before, and I never forget my way about!'

Lowe, slipping off his coat, moved towards the door of the library, and Letitia Delmar went out to the waiting Rolls with White. Lowe, his fingers on the handle of the library door, heard the engine start up again as the car moved off towards the garages at the side of the house. And then, as he was about to open the library door, his whole figure abruptly stiffened.

He had caught sight of something lying against the wall farther along the big, dim-lit hall. Something that lay huddled and still in the shadow of the stairs.

With swift strides, the dramatist hurried across to the foot of the big, old staircase, with its dark, carved banisters and heavy balustrade. Lying there face down in the shadows, one arm outflung as if he had clutched vainly for the support of the balustrade in falling, with a trickle of blood meandering slowly from his chest across the old stone floor, was the figure of a man, clad in a dinner jacket. In another moment the detective was kneeling beside him.

'My God — '

With strong, gentle hands, Lowe turned the iron-grey head. The face of Sir Matthew Moncrieff; and for an instant it seemed to Lowe that the eyelids flickered, that the lips moved a fraction. There came the sound of a long-drawn sigh, followed by a hideous rattle in the throat. The baronet shuddered convulsively, and went limp.

'Moncrieff!' whispered Lowe hoarsely.

But Sir Matthew Moncrieff was dead, with a knife-wound in his chest, above the heart, showing with ghastly clearness the manner of his dying. And Lowe knew now that it had been no fool's errand upon which he and White had driven from London to this lonely old house by the Welsh cliffs.

4

A Shot From the Dark

'Great heavens!'

There was sheer horror in Lowe's face as he rose swiftly to his feet, staring round.

It was clear enough that the blow that had ended the life of Sir Matthew Moncrieff had been struck only a minute or so before, at most; probably even while he and White had been talking with Letitia Delmar in the great doorway at the far side of the hall. So swift and sure had the stroke of the murderer been, that Moncrieff had collapsed without uttering a cry loud enough for them to hear above the restless moan and mutter of the wind that surged round the house. The sound of his fall, too, had been inaudible, thanks to the wind. And so Moncrieff had died unnoticed within forty yards of them — at the stroke of an unseen hand.

The great hall was empty seemingly. No sound but the mutter of the wind and the crackle of the log fire that burnt redly in the cavernous stone fireplace. No one. And yet —

Used though he was to the spectacle of sudden death in all its forms, Lowe felt an icy chill close for a brief moment round his heart.

The bewildering horror of it all appalled him as he stared round, searching the great hall with narrowed eyes. There was a sudden startling crash as the big front door, caught by the wind, slammed shut.

The stairs?

With long strides, Lowe raced up the wide staircase. At the head of them, a long gallery stretched right and left, illuminated with shaded electric lamps set in the walls. No sign of any moving thing.

He hurried down into the hall again. A yellowed tapestry hung on one of the walls near the dead man, and he pulled it down, laying it over the inert form. The dark rill of blood twisting slowly across the stone floor was gathering in a little pool against the stairs.

There was an electric bell-push by the library door. He pressed it; and in a few moments the door at the back of the hall opened and the elderly manservant appeared in answer — a stooping, white-haired figure in a black alpaca coat.

He halted, with an expression of respectful inquiry. And then, as his gaze fell on the shrouded form by the foot of the staircase, his eyes went wide and his mouth opened dumbly. He tried to speak, but the words failed to come.

'Sir Matthew has met with — an accident,' rasped the dramatist. 'A grave accident — '

'He — he is — dead?' The words broke from the old man's lips almost inaudibly.

'Yes. He has been stabbed. He is dead. Murdered.'

'Murder?' The old servant's face was ashen, his hands twitching as he stared down at the vague form outlined beneath the covering tapestry. His eyes saw for the first time the thin trickle of blood and the gathering pool beyond. 'Oh, my God!'

For a moment he seemed to reel. 'But who — who — '

'Are there any other men in the house?' jerked out Lowe. 'We have got to search immediately! The murderer cannot be far away!'

The old man was pulling himself together now with an astonishing display of self-control.

'There is the chauffeur — that's all. And myself — '

'Find the chauffeur!'

'Does — does Miss Letitia know?'

'Not yet.'

The servant hurried away with unsteady steps. Lowe crossed swiftly to the front door — he had heard White and Letitia returning. He opened the door. His secretary and the girl were mounting the steps together; and something in the face of Lowe told them both at the same instant that something was badly wrong.

'What's happened?' jerked out Arnold swiftly.

Lowe's eyes were on the girl as he stepped out on to the steps, drawing the door partly shut behind him.

'Miss Delmar, I have some bad news for you. I want you to be very brave. But you must know. Something terrible has happened. Your uncle — '

'Yes?' she whispered tensely. Her face had gone deathly white, her eyes incredibly startled. 'Tell me — '

'Your uncle has been murdered.'

She stood staring up into the set face of Lowe as if she did not understand — could not understand. Then her clenched hand rose quickly to her mouth, the taut knuckles pressed against her open lips as if to force back the shrill cry of horror that burst from them — an hysterical scream of horror and dread — before her eyes closed and she swayed forward. Lowe caught her in his arms.

He lifted her, carrying her quickly across the threshold into the house, followed by the horrified White. His secretary gave an ejaculation as he caught sight of the shrouded form across the hall.

'What happened?' he jerked out hoarsely.

'Lord knows!' came the grim answer. 'He was knifed. It can only have happened a minute or two ago! Get on the 'phone to the nearest police station. Whoever killed him can't be far away — we must search the house and grounds — '

Arnold White sprang to the telephone that stood on a small table in a recess near the stairs. Lowe carried the senseless girl into the lighted library and laid her on a couch. As he hurried back into the hall, Hurst, the old manservant, was appearing from the kitchen quarters, followed by the chauffeur — a middle-aged man in uniform, stocky and muscular. The face of the chauffeur was a picture of startled horror.

'Get one of the women servants to see to Miss Delmar!' ordered Lowe to the older man. 'She has fainted.' He gripped Hurst by the arm. 'Tell me — what ways out into the gardens are there?'

'There's the back entrance, sir, but I and Rice here were out there, and — '

'Yes, yes — what other ways?'

'Only the garden door, sir, along that passage — and the french windows in the drawing-room. But lately they've been kept locked after dark, sir — and all the windows, too.'

A swift examination proved that not only were all the exits from the house into the grounds fastened on the inside, but that all the ground-floor windows were properly secured.

'Either the murderer has got out of the house by an upstairs window — in which case, with the ground so damp, his footprints where he jumped out are bound to show up well — or he is still in the house!' Lowe was standing in the hall, and there was a Browning automatic in his hand. 'Wait here!'

He swung towards the front door, and they saw him vanish into the darkness outside.

The old manservant slumped into a chair by the big fireplace, as though he had given way suddenly at the knees. He sat staring dazedly in front of him.

'The poor master!' he muttered thickly. 'The poor master! And poor Miss Delmar!'

'If I get my hands on whoever did it — ' broke out the chauffeur savagely.

White was staring up the stairs, listening to the restless murmur of the wind. An air of brooding horror seemed to reign over the ancient building — horror and sinister mystery. Whose had that unseen hand been that had struck down Sir Matthew Moncrieff within only a comparatively few yards of his friends, and then vanished as strangely as it had come, unseen, unheard, like the manifestation of some malignant spirit of evil?

Lowe, hurrying along the path that led round the big old house, the light of an electric torch playing swiftly over the flower-beds that lined the walls, was asking himself the same bewildering question.

That the murderer had been some intruder from without was certain. The strength of the blow that must have been dealt to cause such a wound as that from which Moncrieff had died, proved — if proof were needed — that it had been the work of a man. But the only two men in the house with Moncrieff had been old Hurst and Rice, the chauffeur. Impossible to suspect either of them. Their alibi was unassailable, even if they might otherwise

47

have been suspected; both had been out in the kitchen with the three women servants at the time of the crime.

There was no moon, but there was enough starlight to show the dark gardens that lay round the house, with the windswept trees beyond, and the background of great mountains that rose to the stars in massed ebon piles. The house itself was of stone, its weather-worn walls, grey in the dim starlight, the ancient gables and turrets towering high above the surrounding grounds.

Following the dancing torchlight, Lowe skirted the shadowy walls rapidly, until at last he found himself back at the main entrance. There had been no sign of any footprints indicative of a man's leap from one of the upper windows; it seemed certain that the murderer was still concealed in the house.

Back in the hall, Lowe glanced grimly from Hurst to the chauffeur.

'You two, watch outside — one at the front, the other at the back of the house. Here, take this!' He had taken a police-whistle from his pocket, and handed it to the manservant. 'If you see anyone, or hear Rice shout, blow this whistle for me and my secretary. Meanwhile, we will search the house.'

The body of the murdered man was still lying by the foot of the stairs. Lowe and White lifted it, and gently bore the dead man into a room opening from the hall, where they laid the mortal remains of Sir Matthew Moncrieff upon a low sofa. Returning to the hall, from which Hurst and Rice had already vanished in obedience to Lowe's instructions, the detective glanced at White with flickering eyes.

'Gun handy!' he rasped, and Arnold nodded, 'Good! You may need it. Whoever he is — whatever his motive was in murdering Moncrieff — we're up against something devilish tonight!'

'How did he get in?' muttered the secretary. 'That's what I've been wondering! With all the doors and windows fastened on the inside — '

'I'm wondering the same thing! But there's no time to wonder now. Come on!'

Together they hurried up the wide staircase. All the ground-floor rooms had already been investigated during their examination of doors and windows. If the killer were still at large in the house, it was somewhere in the upper floors.

'With luck, Miss Delmar will be able to throw some light on things as soon as she is fit to discuss it,' said Lowe grimly. They arrived at the first landing, where the long gallery that led to both wings of the house stretched to either side of them — a wide, carpeted corridor hung with pictures; Sir Matthew Moncrieff had been a collector of Dutch interiors. 'You stay here to guard the stairs!'

White nodded and moved into a shadowed alcove, his automatic ready in his hand, the safety-catch thumbed down. He watched Lowe move away along the gallery, searching from room to room.

The house was a large one, and it seemed a long time to Arnold before Lowe returned to the stairs and set off to search the other wing. That search, too, proved fruitless, and together they mounted to the floor above.

The second floor, too, was drawn blank. There were two more floors, and some attics above that. When these had been systematically scoured — without result — they surveyed one another, at the top of the final narrow flight of stairs, with the same thought.

'The roof!' muttered White.

'Looks like it!' agreed Lowe, with a nod.

A trapdoor in a passage near the top of the last flight of stairs gave access to the roofs. It was unfastened, and, with Lowe leading the way, they scrambled out on to the leads.

The wind, laden with the salt tang of the near-by sea, beat gustily into their faces as they stood peering round.

A maze of shadowy parapets and gabled roofs, with great stone chimneys black against the stars, stretched before them. Away to the west the sea could be seen beyond the ragged line of cliffs, dark and stormy.

'Guard this trapdoor, White. If he's up here I'll rout him out!'

Lowe disappeared among the shadowy gables. There were a score of hiding-places there for a fugitive, and the dangerous search would take some time. Arnold, every nerve tense, waited, keenly watchful.

It seemed impossible for the murderer to have escaped from the house, and if he had not done so, Lowe's search of the floors below made it seem certain enough that the unknown killer was concealed somewhere up here. And yet some queer instinct seemed to warn White that Lowe's search of the roofs would prove fruitless — that in some mysterious fashion the murderer of Moncrieff had slipped through their fingers.

His instinct was right. When Lowe returned to the spot where Arnold waited, in the shadow of a giant chimney-stack, it was to announce that he had found the roofs empty.

'What do you make of it?' muttered White.

'Bewildering!' rejoined Lowe grimly.

'Looks as if there must be some sort of a secret door or something in the house,' suggested the secretary. But even as he made the suggestion, he realised that Lowe was not the man to have overlooked such an obvious possibility as that.

Lowe shook his head.

'I was on the look-out for anything of that kind. I'm convinced there's no secret door, or secret panel, to give him entry and exit. He's slipped through our fingers some other way; and I'll find it in the end — '

He broke off, staring across the roofs to the dark stretch of countryside beyond the grounds of the old house. The headlamps of a car had flashed into view, speeding towards the house along the winding, hilly road.

'These are the police, I fancy,' shrugged Lowe. 'They've been pretty quick, considering they've had to come all the way from Caermawr. But they seem to be too late. The bird has apparently flown!'

He returned his gun to his pocket, and Arnold saw the strong hand of Lowe clench remorselessly. He realised how deeply Lowe had been affected by the murder of his old friend — that he would not rest until the murderer was safely in the hands of the law, to pay the grim penalty.

Richards, the Welsh plain-clothes inspector in charge of the three other men who had raced to the house from Caermawr in response to White's urgent telephone call, was a quietly businesslike officer of a type with whom Lowe found co-operation easy. He and his uniformed subordinates made a long search of their own; but it was vain as Lowe's search had been, although there were still no footprints anywhere round the house, which seemingly made it impossible for the murderer to have escaped by way of a window.

The mystery of it was completely baffling, for the time being. But Letitia Delmar was by then sufficiently recovered from the shock of the tragedy to answer their questions; and in the cosy library, with Lowe seated near her and Inspector Richards standing grim-faced by the fireplace, she told the story of the events which had caused her to write with calm courage.

'And your uncle believed these night prowlers to have been gipsies?' asked the dramatist.

The girl nodded. Her face was still very white.

'And the dogs?'

'He supposed they had accidentally picked up something poisonous in the grounds.'

'Certainly, they must have done. But it looks as if whatever they picked up had been put there for them to find,' said the police inspector incisively. 'Now, this figure you thought you saw one night in the gallery on the first floor. Will you explain what you saw in detail?'

'I was going to bed. It was a night about a week ago. My bedroom is on the first floor, in the north wing. I reached the landing, and turned along the gallery, and paused to look at one of the pictures that hang there — it was a new acquisition of my uncle's. He collected pictures. As I turned away from the picture, I saw — or thought I saw — a moving figure at the far end of the gallery. I thought for a moment it was Hurst, the manservant. Then I realised that it was not tall enough for Hurst. Whatever it was, it disappeared almost instantly, as if it had turned into the corridor that runs out of the gallery on the left. I was frightened, and ran downstairs. It was found that all the servants were already in their rooms — none of them had been in the long gallery. Of course, we searched, but we found nobody. My uncle believed that I had imagined it — '

She broke off with a little shiver.

'I can't think it was imagination,' she went on in a low voice. 'And I certainly do not believe in ghosts. But it seemed so impossible for anyone but ourselves and the servants to have been in the house, that I almost let my uncle persuade me I had been imagining things.'

'H'm!' The police officer stroked his moustache dubiously, and glanced at Trevor Lowe.

'How long was it before the discovery of the tragedy that you last saw your uncle?' asked the dramatist after a pause.

'Barely a minute. I was with him when we heard your car. We were in this room. I went out to let you in; and — and then — '

The faltering voice broke off.

'Amazing!' Lowe heard the inspector mutter.

'I think, Miss Delmar, it would be better for you to go away from this house tomorrow, for a while at least,' said Lowe sympathetically. 'I suppose you have some relatives, or friends, with whom you could stay?'

'Yes, I could go to some friends at Shrewsbury. I couldn't stay here! Not now,' she said dully. 'And the house has been sold — '

'Sold?' cut in Lowe quickly.

'My uncle signed the agreement today, so he told me. He knew I wanted to get away, and since an offer was made for the house only the other day — '

'By whom?'

'A French lady, Madame D'Elange.'

'Do you know anything about this lady — this Madame D'Elange?'

'Nothing.' Letitia Delmar shook her head. 'She came here one day and asked if she might look over the house; it is rather historical, you know, and we supposed that was the reason she was interested. She was quite young, and very good-looking. I showed her round the place myself. And a day or two later we had an offer for the house, through an agent, and found it was from Madame D'Elange. My uncle said it was a surprisingly high price that she offered.'

'Who were the agents?'

'Chambers & Sons, of Berkeley Street, London.'

'Thank you.' Lowe took out a pocket-book and made a scribbled note of the name. He glanced at the inspector. 'Might be worthwhile interviewing Madame D'Elange,' was the unvoiced comment revealed by his glance.

There was a tap on the door, and Arnold entered the room.

'I've found this,' he said briefly. 'Out in the grounds.'

Lowe took the object that his secretary held out. It was a gold watch, without a glass, its face broken, and some of the works visible — badly rusted. Evidently it had been exposed to the weather for some days at least.

'Thought it might prove to be of some use,' added White. 'Struck me as rather a surprising find. It's not often people leave gold watches lying about out of doors! I happened to spot it among the bushes by the french windows of the drawing-room.'

Lowe turned the broken watch over in his hand, and glanced at Letitia Delmar.

'Was this your uncle's property, Miss Delmar?'

The pale-faced girl seated near him shook her head. Lowe was trying to open the back of the watch, but for some moments it stuck obstinately, then it clicked open. Until then, the dramatist's expression had been casual enough; now it changed abruptly.

White, looking down over his shoulder, saw that a tiny label was affixed to the inner side of the back of the watch — a label that bore some peculiar signs that looked to him like Chinese. He heard Lowe draw a quick breath.

'You've found something, Mr. Lowe?' exclaimed the police officer, and the dramatist nodded.

'Yes,' he answered slowly, and his eyes turned to White. 'White — of all the amazing things! This watch belonged to the captain of the *Oki Maru*!'

'By Jove!' Arnold stared down into

Lowe's queerly flickering eyes almost incredulously. 'You mean to say — '

'The *Oki Maru?*' broke in the inspector, bewildered.

'A Japanese steamer that sailed from Liverpool a month or so ago and disappeared at sea,' nodded Lowe. For the moment he did not offer further details — that the Korean second mate was 'wanted' by Scotland Yard for the murder of a compatriot in the midnight express to Liverpool, or the strange story of the chronometer of the lost ship. 'Show me just where you found this, Arnold!'

White turned towards the door without questioning Lowe's amazing statement. The puzzled inspector followed them from the room, and White crossed to the front door and swung it open.

'This is going to surprise Shadgold!' muttered Arnold wonderingly. 'This beats everything!'

He was leading the way quickly down the steps. The wind had dropped a little, and everything was very quiet in the dark grounds, an almost eerie, brooding hush — broken suddenly in startling fashion.

Out of the darkness somewhere to their right a sinister pencil of flame had leapt, instantaneous, with a staccato report — the crack of an automatic. A bullet whined past Lowe's head, and buried itself with a thud in the heavy woodwork of the big door.

Arnold's words snapped off, and the three froze where they stood. Lowe was the first to act.

'Look out!' he rapped.

He leapt back up the steps, grasped the old arched door, and slammed it shut with an echoing crash.

For the moment, at least, all thought of the mysterious clue that White had discovered in the garden was dismissed from their minds. At any instant they expected another bullet to come out of the darkness, even though now, thanks to Lowe's swift shutting of the door behind them, the light of the hall was blotted out, against which they had been outlined so clearly as a target for the hidden marksman.

In another moment or two the three of them had leapt down the steps, were

61

standing pressed back against the house wall, invisible now to the unseen man whose shot from the opposite trees had so nearly found a billet.

The shot was not repeated. Lowe snatched the gun from his pocket and thumbed down the safety-catch. He laughed harshly.

'Our unseen sportsman nearly got me, by thunder! Well, I'm still alive. And now I'd like to get him!'

'Who the devil was it?' asked White.

He, too, had taken the gun from his pocket, was peering across the wide stone-flagged courtyard and the lawns beyond, towards the dim patch of deeper darkness that was all they could see of the little plantation of windswept trees from which the mysterious shot had come.

At the head of the broad stone steps the big door was flung open and a glare of light streamed out past them. One of the inspector's men came running out. He had heard the shot, and the bullet that had thudded into the heavy old door. He was followed by the other two of Richards' subordinates, the latter halting on the steps, peering down.

'Shut that door!' snarled the inspector savagely, and his tone was such that the door was hastily slammed, without a second bidding. The three policemen came running down the steps.

'Inspector, take your men round to the back of the plantation as quick as you can make it! Use the cover of that hedge there! Cut off his retreat to the gates, if you can! We've got to get the man that fired that shot!'

Without waiting for the inspector to reply, Lowe broke into a run across the courtyard towards the plantation. White at his side.

It was a dangerous manoeuvre, open as they were to the gun-fire of the man hidden among those dark trees. But in the shadowy starlight it would take a skilful marksman to pick them off with an automatic, and Lowe was taking chances in his determination to get his man.

It was not his habit to reveal much emotion as general rule, but that did not mean that he failed to feel as deeply — perhaps more deeply — than the average man. And the murder of his old friend, Moncrieff, had stirred him to a savagely relentless resolve, a fierce, settled purpose to bring the murderer to justice at any cost.

That there was a bewildering mystery mixed up with the death of Sir Matthew Moncrieff he realised well enough, though as yet they had only touched the fringe of the riddle, a mystery that seemed, amazingly enough, as though it might prove to have some queer connection with that other mystery of which Shadgold had spoken only that day in his office at Scotland Yard — the problem surrounding the vanished Japanese steamer, the *Oki Maru*, and its murderous second mate. But whatever strange facts might ultimately come to light as lying behind the events that had occurred at this lonely house, Lowe's whole being was centred upon bringing to justice the murderer of Letitia Delmar's uncle; and whether or not the man who had fired from the plantation was that murderer, it was evident enough that the hidden marksman would prove a valuable capture in the elucidation of the grim mystery surrounding the house.

Their running footsteps all but sound-less on the soft grass, Lowe and White raced across the wide lawn, guns ready, eyes peering tensely ahead. But still there was no sign from the trees, and they gained the dark shadow of the plantation without another shot having been fired.

It was pitch-black under the trees. Above their heads, as they halted among the shadowy tree-trunks, the oak branches rustled softly in the wind from the sea. An owl hooted mournfully and glided away on silent wings. It occurred to White that this was the plantation where the poi-soned dogs had been found. A queerly eerie spot by night at any time, but with the knowledge that an armed killer was probably lurking somewhere within easy distance of them a grim place indeed.

They listened. No sound other than the sigh of the wind.

If, after firing that single shot, the hidden man had decided to clear, there seemed every chance that he might fall into the hands of Richards and his men, whom Lowe had dispatched to cut off the unknown's possible retreat towards the gate. If he had remained where he was, believing that they would not dare attack directly across the open lawns, he must be very close to them. With a touch on White's arm, Lowe moved forward with flickering eyes, his finger resting lightly on the trigger of his Browning, searching the darkness for any sign of a crouching figure among the close-set trees.

Opening out from one another as they went, the two stole forward, footsteps silent on the carpet of damp leaves.

A faint movement somewhere to his left caused Lowe to turn quickly in that direction. He slipped into the cover offered by the trunk of a twisted oak, eyes straining into the gloom. White had vanished in the other direction.

The sound was not repeated, and Lowe stole on, alert, tensely watchful. In the dead darkness, this dangerous blindfold game was a reckless gamble enough — called for a knife-edge concentration of all the senses, with a killer seemingly at bay.

By now the four police officers must have made their flanking movement, he knew. If the unknown man realised that he was in a net —

A sudden movement within a yard or two of his left hand brought him swinging round in a flash. Out of the gloom a darker shadow had appeared from the shelter of one of the trees — a dark, leaping shadow that was already on him. Before Lowe could bring his gun round his body in time to shoot, something crashed down upon his head with sickening, stunning force.

He reeled, stumbled, half-stunned, to his knees, the automatic slipping from his momentarily-dulled grasp, and then powerful fingers came twining round his throat, digging deep into the flesh.

The uncanny silence of that swift attack had given no indication to White, now at the other side of the plantation, of what was happening. It was a man-to-man fight between Lowe and the shadowy unknown, and all the advantage with the attacker.

Somehow he managed to fight to his feet, although the steely savage fingers still held his throat in their relentless grasp. With senses still dazed and reeling, a sickening thudding in his brain, the dramatist struggled to free himself from that vice-like grip about his windpipe. But, powerful though he was, he realised that on this occasion he had met his equal.

It was no time for fancy fighting. A knee in the other's stomach, a smashing uppercut to the unseen face, delivered with amazing force considering his dazed, half-throttled state, freed him at last from the strangling grip about his throat. Again he slammed home with his clenched right, but the shadowy figure avoided the blow and leapt in.

Lowe staggered as a swinging left-hander crashed in between his eyes. Whoever the man was, there was that in his method of meeting Lowe's return attack that proclaimed the Anglo-Saxon. Lowe had more than half expected to feel a knife tearing in between his ribs. But the other had met him with bare fists, surprisingly enough.

It was like fighting a shadow — a

powerful, very tangible shadow.

Muscular arms came winging round him, panting breath beat upon his face. A hand came groping for his throat. But Lowe gripped the sinewy wrist, and with a ju-jitsu trick that must almost have broken his enemy's arm he flung his attacker from him. As he did so his foot met something hard — his fallen automatic.

Stooping swiftly, he snatched up the weapon. As he straightened himself, a savage blow in the face sent him reeling. But the gun was in his hand now, and as his shadowy antagonist came leaping at him Lowe slammed the cold steel circle in against the man's stomach.

That the other recognised the force of that grim argument was evident. He froze motionless, and Lowe laughed savagely.

'Move an inch, and I'll blow a hole in your middle the size of a smokestack!' he muttered. 'I mean that! And I'll just take a look at you!'

Already his left hand was groping in his pocket for the flash-lamp that lay there. He snatched it out and directed a blinding white ray into the face of his captive. As he did so, he heard White running through the trees. Apparently the secretary had heard the all-but-silent struggle at last.

Automatic pressed hard into the other's stomach, the light of his electric torch flooding the man's face with a white glare, Lowe stood staring, incredibly amazed.

'You!' he breathed.

For the grim face, with its queer pale-blue eyes and rugged jaw, was that of a man he knew well — 'No 55,' of the British Secret Service — otherwise Michael Dene.

5

Mr. Tsu

'Dene!'

'Satisfied with your capture, Lowe?'

There was a note of dry amusement in the deep voice, a crooked smile on the face of the Secret Service man — a face that bore more than a few traces of their blindfold struggle. But Lowe, too, had escaped far from unscathed.

'Talk about dog eating dog!' chuckled Dene, a trifle wryly. 'Never recognised you till you spoke just now! I thought you were — well, someone I've an ache against.' He paused, with another deep chuckle. 'I meant to knock the fight out of you, instead of which — ' He shrugged his powerful shoulders. 'Your win, I think!'

They gripped hands in the darkness. Lowe had lowered his torch. White, who had arrived on the scene by now, had recognised Dene with as much astonishment as Lowe had done a few moments before.

'What on earth are you doing here, Dene?' muttered Lowe, peering into the shadowy, half-invisible face of the Secret Service man.

'A little job of work for the Department!' came the laconic answer.

'Who fired that shot?' jerked out Lowe swiftly. 'Someone fired from among those trees — nearly outed me as I was coming out of the house — '

'Did I? Lord, I never realised anything of that! My best apologies. Yes, it was I who fired. I was here, watching the house. Someone turned up as if from nowhere, and attacked me. I fired at him, and the bullet must have gone on to where you were. Looks like a narrow escape from having your blood on my hands!'

'A narrow shave for me all right,' nodded Lowe grimly. 'But I don't understand! Who — '

'Who was I firing at? Only wish I knew! He attacked me with a knife — then vanished, after I'd let the lead fly.

I thought you were he, back again; or one of his pals. Look here, Lowe, what's brought you here, anyhow?'

Lowe flung out a pointing hand towards the grim old turreted house.

'There's been murder in that house tonight, Dene. In the last hour! Whoever attacked you here, looks like having been the murderer! He's the fellow we're hunting — '

'Then I fancy you're too late, Lowe. Whoever he was, the sportsman with the knife has made his get-away, it's a safe bet. I only hope I'm wrong, for I'm as interested in him as you are — for my own reasons. If he is still around, we'll hunt him out all right!' Already they were hurrying out from the plantation. 'You say he's done murder here?'

'Yes. Sir Matthew Moncrieff — poor devil.'

He heard Dene's startled ejaculation in the gloom.

They emerged from the trees into the dim starlight of the paddock at the back of the plantation. Inspector Richards came hurrying up. Lowe gave a terse explanation of Dene's presence; and the fact that he was a friend of the dramatist's was sufficient for the police officer. In answer to a swift question, Richards shook his head.

'No, sir; no sign of anyone.'

'He can't be far,' grunted White.

'No. But he's a swift mover, whoever he is!' rasped Dene sardonically. 'It's my opinion he's made a get-away!'

His words were justified. An intensive search of the grounds revealed no sign of their mysterious quarry. Lowe's face was grim and thoughtful as they made their way at last back into the house.

Letitia Delmar had gone to her room, an old woman servant who had been her nurse as a child being with her. The arrival of the police surgeon from Caermawr took the inspector into the room where the murdered man lay, and Lowe, White and Dene entered the library alone.

'What about some mutual explanations, Dene?' suggested Lowe. 'I don't know how secret your present job is, but since we both seem to be mixed up with

74

the same affair — '

'Fire away!' agreed Dene laconically. He was lighting a scarred bulldog briar filled with tobacco so strong that it would have 'fumigated an elephant-house,' as White remarked, his tall, big-boned figure radiating strength and energy as he moved restlessly to and fro across the floor.

In terse sentences, Lowe explained the reason for their presence at the house, and the events that had followed their arrival. Dene's queer, compelling blue eyes began to gleam oddly as he listened. As Lowe finished, he plucked the pipe from his lips, and nodded.

'Interesting!' he murmured. 'Thundering interesting! Particularly — to me — this business of the Japanese steamer — the *Oki Maru*. It seems to link in with my own job most uncommonly. You see, I happen to be interested in things Japanese at the moment!'

His words were almost the same as those which Shadgold had employed at Scotland Yard that morning with regard to him. But Lowe had not mentioned what Shadgold had told him concerning Dene — that had been in confidence.

'A draft of the proposed treaty between this country and Japan was stolen by some person or persons unknown from a safe in the Foreign Office, a short time ago,' went on Dene. He was pacing the floor slowly, his big, muscular form, clad in a suit that bore the obvious cut of Savile Row — though certainly without any foppishness about him — made a commanding figure in the softly-lit room. 'The newspapers got hold of the yarn, and made a thundering row. Well, believe me, even the newspapers don't realise just how serious the theft of that treaty is!'

He halted, fastening a pair of hard, flickering eyes on Lowe.

'We don't know who stole that draft treaty, Lowe. But if it gets into the wrong hands — to put it that way — it may mean — well, almost anything — '

'What do you mean by that?'

'War. That's what I mean, Lowe. Yes — war!'

'England?'

'Oh, yes, England would be in it! You

know what these international treaties are. Harmless enough, so long as they don't go astray! When they do go astray, the results are sometimes uncontrollable. Look at the Big War — it began in a small enough way, just Austria and Serbia. Little things lead to big things, these days — like lighting a match in a petrol store! Still, we needn't go into that. Enough to know that at any cost that draft treaty has got to be recovered. Got to be! No two words about it. It must be recovered!'

'What are the chances?'

'Difficult to answer that. All I can say for certain is that I am on a certain trail. A woman's trail!'

'A woman's trail!' ejaculated Lowe swiftly. His thoughts leapt to what he had been told by Letitia Delmar regarding the sale of the house — the unknown Madame D'Elange, who had purchased the place for what Sir Matthew Moncrieff had considered a surprisingly high price.

'Yes, a woman, Lowe! An old friend of ours. Mademoiselle Julie!'

'Mademoiselle Julie!' muttered the dramatist. 'She's in it?'

'She's in it, so I believe,' nodded Dene, with a slow smile.

Lowe's expression had changed.

Mademoiselle Julie, the most trusted agent of the French Secret Service, whose beauty and wits made her one of the most dangerous opponents any man could face, was an old acquaintance of Lowe's, as she was of Dene's. Sometimes circumstances had been such that the French girl had worked with Dene, when the interests of the French Secret Service had been allied with those of Whitehall; more often, she had worked against him — and it was said of her that Dene was the only man in the Service whose abilities she remotely feared or even respected.

A queer relationship had grown up between them; as a rule implacable foes — yet friends as well. Lowe knew that Dene, the last man in the world to be in any degree sentimental, not only respected the French girl spy as a foeman worthy of his steel, but had in his heart a very warm corner for her as a woman.

'Where does Julie come in?' he asked abruptly.

'The French Government is known to be thundering keen on getting hold of that stolen treaty.' The deep voice of the Secret Service man was quiet and casual enough, but the expression in his eyes told Lowe how much it meant to Dene to foil that ambition on the part of the Quai D'Orsay. 'It was discovered by one of our men over in Paris that Mlle. Julie was being sent over here to find out what had happened to it — and to get it! Julie came over — of course, under another name, with a false passport, and was followed all the way over by our agent. He thought she didn't know he was trailing her. But Julie didn't miss much! She gave him the slip in Edinburgh, after leading him a pretty dance all over the country — made a complete fool of him. After that, she vanished. Well, I got on her trail in the end — never mind how for the moment — and hung on to her every movement like her own shadow. Luckily she didn't know she was being watched this time! And Julie's trail led me to this house. She came here several times, though mostly she only seemed to be examining the lie of the land. One day she charged in as bold as brass, though I don't know on what pretext. Knowing Julie, it's obvious she didn't trek out here for the good of her complexion! She must believe, rightly or wrongly, that this house has some connection with the job she is working on, the little matter of this stolen Anglo-Japanese treaty!'

'Obviously,' agreed Lowe.

'I came here tonight alone, to take a look round for myself,' went on Dene. 'If Julie is on the trail of that draft treaty — and, by thunder, I'll swear she is — I'll soon be on it, too!'

'I think I can tell you something that will interest you, Dene! A certain French lady, a Madame D'Elange, who recently visited this house, has bought it, insisting upon immediate occupation. Poor Moncrieff fixed the sale today, the the lady takes possession tomorrow. It's quite evident, from what you've said, that this so-called Madame D'Elange is Julie herself.'

'What!' Michael Dene jerked the pipe from his lips. 'Julie has bought this house?

Comes here tomorrow? Jove! What the deuce does it mean?'

'I should be as interested to know as you!' responded Lowe grimly. 'There would seem to be some connection between this house and that lost Japanese steamer; and it's beginning to look as though there is some connection between the *Oki Maru* and the stolen treaty! A watch belonging to the captain has been found here in the grounds. How it all fits in is the deuce of a problem — at present.'

'How did you know that watch belonged to the captain of the *Oki Maru*?' cut in Dene.

'The Japanese characters inside the case told me so. I have a fair smattering of Japanese, and of the characters in which it is written. 'Shasataka, Captain, *Oki Maru*,' is the translation of the characters on the label inside the back of this watch.'

Lowe had taken the watch in question from his pocket and was examining it again, minutely.

'Well, that seems conclusive enough,' growled Dene, raising a hand to rub his jaw, where a darkening bruise showed the force with which one of Lowe's blows had been dealt during their struggle in the plantation.

The police surgeon entered the room, a dapper little Welshman, with gold-rimmed pince-nez. Though his visit had been necessary for official purposes, his examination of the dead baronet had been entirely formal; the cause of Sir Matthew Moncrieff's death had only been too grimly evident, even though the circumstances that lay behind it were still so mysterious. Inspector Richards accompanied the medical man into the room.

'This is a very queer business, sir,' volunteered the inspector, and Dene smiled sardonically.

'A thundering sight more queer than you suppose, I fancy — '

He broke off abruptly. From somewhere in the house a sudden shrill scream had echoed piercingly, to snap off as sharply as it had begun.

The little medical man started violently.

'What was that?' he cried.

Already Dene was at the door. He dragged it open, and ran out into the hall, Lowe close behind him, the others following. The scream seemed to have come from somewhere above; and with giant strides Dene tore up the staircase.

'Good God!'

The Secret Service man had reached the long gallery. But he was not the first. A uniformed figure, that of a police-constable who had been stationed in the hall and had raced up the stairs ahead of them in response to that shrill scream from above, was already in the gallery — staring wide-eyed at a crumpled figure that lay there, lit by the soft glow of the wall-lamps; the figure of a girl, eyes closed, face deathly white, lying huddled on the rug-strewn polished floor before one of the old paintings that hung in the galley.

Trevor Lowe, staring past the big, muscular figure of the Secret Service man, drew a swift, startled breath.

The huddled figure was that of Letitia Delmar; and written across the face of the big picture on the wall behind her, daubed there with some white pigment by an unknown hand, was a group of strange hieroglyphics — Japanese characters, weirdly picturesque, yet, in these circumstances, strangely sinister.

Arnold White, Inspector Richards, and the police surgeon were hurrying up the staircase; already the constable was bending anxiously over the quiet form in the gallery, and there was keen relief in his face as he glanced up.

'She's not dead,' he said hoarsely. 'Looks like she's fainted.'

'But — but what in the world — ' began the police surgeon excitedly. He caught sight of the cryptic characters written across the picture on the wall, and flung out a shaking hand. 'Look! Look! What's that?'

'Never mind what that is!' cried Dene fiercely. 'Take a look at this girl!'

Almost by physical force he hauled the scared little medical man along the gallery. Lowe himself was examining the still figure, but he drew aside from deference to the surgeon's profession, though he had already made up his mind regarding the unconscious condition of Letitia Delmar. With a nervous glance round him, the medical man bent over her.

'There is no sign of any violence,' he stammered after a quick examination. 'It is simply a faint.'

The memory of that shrill scream was still very vivid in the minds of all. Dene glanced at Lowe with smouldering eyes.

'A faint, eh? But what did she see to make her faint? And to make her scream like that? What did she see?'

Lowe was staring across at the daubed Japanese characters on the picture opposite.

'I think I know what she saw, Dene. She saw the man who wrote that!'

'What is it?' muttered Dene. 'What's it mean? Can you read it?'

'Enough to judge what it means,' nodded Lowe. 'It is Japanese. 'Aki karasu — ''

'But in English?'

'In English, roughly: 'This evening the crow has visited this house. It will come again.''

There was a bewildered silence as the little group of startled men stared wonderingly at the writing on the picture. Lowe stepped up to it and touched the daubed Japanese lettering.

'Coarse white paint,' he said. 'And still wet!' His eyes met Dene's. 'There is someone in this house tonight as well as ourselves — '

'But what the devil do those words mean?' jerked out the Secret Service man. ' "The crow has visited this house — " '

'A threat!' cut in Lowe. ' "Karasu" — the crow — a bird of ill-omen, the symbol of death. The meaning is plain. 'Death has come to this house tonight. It will come again!" '

White was kneeling beside the senseless girl, supporting her head. Letitia Delmar's face was still deathly pale, utterly drained of blood, her breathing slow and laboured.

Through the window at the far end of the gallery, where the curtains were only partly drawn, the towering mountains that closed in upon the house on the northern side were darkly visible by the light of the newly risen moon. A strange, brooding menace seemed to fill the house. Lowe's quietly spoken words were echoing in the minds of all: 'There is someone in this house tonight as well as ourselves!'

'Looks as if we didn't hunt well enough, after all, inspector!' Lowe was the first to break the silence. 'Yet I could have sworn — '

'We'll hunt again!' nodded the inspector grimly. 'Whoever wrote those Japanese characters there, is in the house — now! That's certain!'

'Can it have been one of the servants?' muttered White. But even as he made the suggestion, he realised how utterly unlikely it was.

'Miss Delmar had better be carried to her room,' said Lowe incisively. 'Arnold, see if you can find one of the women servants, will you, to look after her?'

White nodded, and hurried down the stairs, crossing the big hall below in the direction of the kitchen quarters. Lowe and Dene lifted the unconscious girl between them, and bore her along to the room which they knew to be hers. The doctor remained with her; and Lowe, Dene and the inspector returned to where the constable stood at the head of the staircase, his eyes still fastened uneasily upon the weird characters daubed across the face of the big picture on the wall — that strange message in Japanese that had appeared there so uncannily, with its sinister significance.

'What now, Lowe?' rasped Dene.

Before Lowe could reply, a sudden loud knocking on the front door echoed through the big hall beneath.

'Who the devil's this?' muttered Dene.

'We'll soon find out!' answered Lowe, tersely.

He strode down the stairs, and across the hall to the main door. Dene, Richards and the constable followed to the foot of the staircase, and halted, staring across. Lowe flung the big door wide open.

Framed in the arched opening, lit by the glow of light that streamed out on to the steps, was a gross, corpulent figure, immaculately clad in silk hat and snowy spats, with a luxurious fur-collared greatcoat; a man whose fleshy brown-yellow face and sleepy black almond eyes were smiling blandly as he stepped silently across the threshold into the hall.

'Good evening.' The voice was perfect in its English. 'I wish to see Sir Matthew Moncrieff. Here is my card.'

He produced a gold-mounted pocket-case and extracted a visiting-card, handing it with fleshy fingers to Trevor Lowe.

The dramatist took it, and read the name engraved upon it:

Mr. Tsu Ni,
101, Berkeley Square,
London, W.I.

6

The Capture

'I have come to see Sir Matthew Moncrieff.'

The words were bland and smooth as the yellow-brown face of the speaker.

The newcomer did not seem to have noticed the uniformed constable; or, if he had, to have realised that the constable's presence indicated anything out of the ordinary. With his glossy silk hat balanced carefully in his gloved hand, eyes queerly inscrutable, Mr. Tsu Ni stood surveying Lowe with a suave smile on his moon-like countenance.

White had appeared again in the hall, crossing to where Dene stood near the foot of the staircase with the inspector and the constable. And White, as he surveyed the stout figure in the luxurious fur-collared coat, recalled inwardly Lowe's startling translation of the words daubed in Japanese characters on the picture in the long gallery: 'Death has come to this house tonight. It will come again!'

Could it be that this Oriental figure himself personified that cryptic threat?

'You are a friend of Sir Matthew's, Mr. Ni?'

The dramatist was asking the question in casual tones. But his eyes never left the fat yellow face.

'Not at all.' Mr. Ni shook his smoothly brushed head smilingly. 'I am afraid it is a little late for my visit. But I have driven from London, and the car — er — broke down.' He gestured towards the open door. A car was visible, drawn up at the foot of the steps, a chauffeur seated, immobile, at the wheel. 'Having come so far, I trusted that Sir Matthew would graciously see me. My business? Simply that I understand this house is for sale. Chambers & Sons, the agents, of Berkeley Street, told me so. If I might see Sir Matthew — '

The smooth words broke off. He glanced inquiringly towards the group by the foot of the stairs, as if wondering if

Dene were the baronet.

The Secret Service man strolled forward. His peculiar blue eyes were very intent upon the newcomer.

'You are too late, Mr. Ni,' he said slowly.

'Too late?'

'The house was sold today.'

A queer flicker seemed to leap up for an instant in the black eyes of Ni, and vanished swiftly. He made a smiling gesture.

'How sad!' He was surveying Dene with veiled keenness. 'You, perhaps, are Sir Matthew Moncrieff himself?'

'No.' A harsh note crept into Dene's voice. 'Sir Matthew Moncrieff is — dead!'

He rapped out the final word like a pistol shot. But if he hoped to startle the Oriental into a betraying sign of any kind, he was disappointed. Not a muscle of the yellow-brown face moved.

'But I was given to understand by the agents — ' began Ni suavely.

'Sir Matthew Moncrieff died only an hour or two ago.' It was Lowe who spoke. 'He was murdered. Here in this house.'

Nothing, however, seemed to have power to alter the expressionless suavity on the face of Mr. Ni. Thoughtfully he glanced at the police constable, as if at last understanding the reason for his presence, though seemingly quite unruffled by the grim information.

'How sadly unfortunate!' he murmured gravely.

'Very!' agreed Michael Dene dryly. 'As you see, for the time being the house is in the hands of the police.'

'Ah! I understand. You gentlemen are police officers?' He paused expectantly. But neither answered the question, and he went on, 'In that case, I fear my long journey has been in vain. Goodnight, gentlemen!'

With a formal bow, Mr. Ni turned and passed out on to the steps, descending to the waiting car. Lowe gestured swiftly to White; and the secretary, understanding, raced silently across the hall and along a passage that led to a garden door. He slipped through into the darkness of the courtyard, and stood pressed back in the shadows — waiting.

In a few moments, the hum of the Oriental's car came to his ears, and the light of dimmed headlamps splashed past him. White, invisible in the dark, narrow doorway, waited motionless until the car passed abreast of him as it turned slowly towards the drive that led to the gates. Then, with an agile leap, he sprang for the luggage-grid, hauled himself on to it as the car gathered speed.

He grinned to himself as the car accelerated, speeding down the long oak-lined drive towards the distant gates. His perch was uncomfortable enough; but he was ready to remain where he was for a hundred miles or more if necessary. In obedience to Lowe's silent instructions, he was going to hang on to the mysterious Mr. Ni like a leech — find out all he could about this man with the bland yellow face who had wished to buy, so he said, the house where Matthew Moncrieff had died.

The car slowed down as it reached the high iron gates, set between shadowy stone pillars; swung out into the road, and accelerated once more, leaping away towards the hill road that joined the main road to London.

Arnold settled himself as comfortably as possible on his narrow perch, his back resting against the dark, polished back of the car's body, watching the dim road stream away behind him as the big car raced on — at nearer sixty miles an hour than fifty, he judged, despite the tortuous bends.

It must have been four miles or so from the old house that the car slowed down and turned into a narrow lane, mounting steeply between desolate rock-strewn slopes. White gave a mutter of surprise. So Ni was not making for the London road after all!

All his previous suspicions of the man — suspicions shared, he knew, by both Lowe and Dene — leapt to life instantly. This narrow lane, winding up towards the mountains that frowned down from high against the stars, seemingly led nowhere, unless to some small farm or tiny mountain village. For what conceivable reason could Mr. Ni, of London, have instructed his chauffeur to go this way?

The wheels of the heavy car were churning noisily among the treacherous loose stones that surfaced the lane. Higher and higher up the hillside; and White, glancing down, saw that now the ruby rear-light of the car was out. That meant that the headlamps were out as well, that the car was travelling now without lights.

The reason seemed evident. The steep hillside was almostly directly opposite Moncrieff's house, and plainly visible from there. Ni, it seemed, was taking precautions lest the route he had taken should be seen by those at the house.

Steeper and steeper the lane grew, twisting tortuously, the powerful car grinding noisily in bottom gear as it climbed. Far beneath, the old house where Moncrieff had died that night — murdered by an unknown hand — was vaguely visible in the starlight. White could see two lighted windows, yellow and unwinking, very tiny at that distance. Beyond, the ragged line of cliffs, a quarter of a mile or so from the house, stood out black against the glimmering sea that stretched to the far, sweeping immensity of the horizon.

Where was Ni making for? A bewildering riddle — but one that he seemed well on the way to finding out.

The lane twisted sharply. In another hundred yards the car came to an abrupt standstill, at a point where the narrow road had flattened out. White heard doors opening as both the chauffeur and his master jumped out.

The halt had been so abrupt that Arnold had no time to slip from the luggage-grid and seek a place of better concealment; and now, with Ni and the driver standing in the road only a few yards from him, to have stirred from where he crouched on the metal grid would have meant certain detection. He huddled against the back of the car, motionless, straining his ears.

Ni and the chauffeur were talking together in low voices, their words inaudible above the blustering wind that tore across the hillside, rustling noisily through the low bushes that crowned the steep, stony bank to the left of the lane. But it seemed to White that the two men were talking in English. And then, in a sudden momentary lull of the wind, he heard the voice of Ni — no longer smooth and suave, as it had been at the house, but coldly malignant:

'Yes, Michael Dene! Without doubt! I tell you — '

So the man's pretence of believing Dene to be a police officer had been nothing but a blind. Ni had recognised him, had known him from the first.

The low talk ceased. White heard Ni take something from the interior of the car, and move away. Cautiously he peered round the back of the stationary vehicle, and saw the stout figure in the heavy fur-collared overcoat and glossy silk hat — so strangely incongruous, on this wild, lonely hillside — clambering with surprising agility up the stony bank that edged the lane. He was carrying something in his hand, something that looked like a small square box with a metal handle from which it was slung.

The chauffeur was waiting by the car, lighting a cigarette. The tiny flame of the match, flung back by his cupped hands, revealed his face — a white man, lean, lantern-jawed.

Ni had gained the top of the bank and

halted there, a bulky figure, black against the stars. He seemed to be staring down the hillside, the square box held now in both hands.

From this part of the hillside the lonely old house near the cliffs was invisible, cut off from view by a dark shoulder of hill. As Arnold watched, peering round the back of the car, he saw a thin beam of light come leaping from the thing in Ni's hands, piercing the darkness with a vivid pencil-thin ray.

He realised now that it was a powerful electric lamp that Ni held. The narrow ray went out abruptly, leapt forth again, flickering in a swift series of long and short flashes.

Ni was signalling to someone far away below, and after a few moments an answering point of light flickered brightly out of the darkness in evident reply. It seemed to White that the answering signal came from somewhere on the cliffs by the sea-edge. The far-off point of light flashed jerkily, while Ni stood motionless, watching.

If it were Morse Code, the signals were

either in a foreign tongue or were forming into code words, for White could make nothing of the flickering flashes, expert reader of Morse though he was. The far-off light on the cliffs went out finally, and once more Ni's powerful-lensed lamp leapt to life, stabbing the darkness of the hillside with its intermittent code.

Whatever these signals meant they were invisible to those in the house Ni had recently left. That, clearly, was why he had come to this spot. From here he could signal to whoever it was with whom he was in touch, without the fact being known.

His signals ended as abruptly as they had begun. For an instant the distant answering light flickered back, as if in acknowledgment of the message. Ni turned and came scrambling back down the bank towards the car.

A sudden startled ejaculation near him caused Arnold to turn his head swiftly. He had been watching Ni so intently that for the moment he had forgotten the chauffeur, and now, it seemed, the latter had walked round to the back of the car as if to examine the road with a view to turning his vehicle. The secretary found two narrow, malignant eyes peering at him with astonished consternation, and the next instant the chauffeur's hand had leapt to his pocket with a quick movement, at the same moment that a hoarse, warning shout broke from him.

White leapt into the road, his hand flashing for his gun. His fingers closed upon it, where it lay in the side-pocket of his jacket, and he fired through the cloth at the same moment that the lean chauffeur whipped up the dully-gleaming automatic that had appeared in his gaunt fist.

A tongue of flame tore through White's pocket.

It was point-blank range, and with a sobbing cry the chauffeur reeled, his weapon blazing harmlessly into the road as his hand dropped loosely, Arnold's bullet embedded in his shoulder. Earth and stones flew up, rattling against the back of the car, stinging White's face, as the chauffeur's bullet tore the surface of the road, and then fat, cold hands, strangely clammy, fastened round his throat from behind.

He tried to twist round and grapple with this attack from the rear. But the man, whose fat, repellent fingers were digging into his throat, seemed, despite his corpulence, to be possessed of gorilla strength. The gun was twisted from his hand, a forearm came sliding round his neck, locked tight, dragging him back, and a malevolent voice whispered purringly in his ear:

'So clever, my friend — so clever, and so curious! But curiosity is dangerous — '

With a supreme effort White succeeded somehow in twisting round to meet his assailant, despite that deadly lock upon his neck. The fat yellow face with the evil eyes was like some baleful mask as it glared into his own, utterly inhuman in its cold malignancy.

Arnold slammed a fist for the smooth yellow face. Had it landed Ni would have gone down like a felled ox, for all White's strength was behind that blow. But the evil figure evaded it with an agility uncanny in a man of his heavy frame, and the next moment something crashed down upon the secretary's head from behind. The chauffeur, blood dripping down his right arm from his wounded shoulder, had staggered forward and struck him across the back of the head with the butt of the big automatic now clutched in his left hand; and White, reeling dazedly, felt Ni's fat fingers fastened again upon his throat with all their amazing strength.

Dazedly he tried to fight free. Out of the haze that swam before his eyes the grinning, evil eyes of Mr. Ni glared out like black polished stones. The yellow fingers were dug deep into his neck.

A second time the lean chauffeur crashed the heavy automatic down on White's head. He slumped into the road without a sound.

'Let me blow his brains out,' snarled the chauffeur venomously.

He half-raised his weapon. Ni gave him a cold, steady look that caused the man to lower it again, muttering.

'Is it for you to say what shall be done with him, Fabian, or is it for me to say?'

The words were gentle, almost caressing, but there was something in the purring tones — a note of ice-cold savagery — that caused the chauffeur to draw back.

'He plugged me!' he muttered.

'I am glad that he did so — before you had time to shoot him. You are a fool, Fabian! I want this man.'

The Korean — though London was his home, Mr. Tsu Ni was Korean — stooped and raised the senseless figure of White as though it had no more weight than a child's. He flung the inert form into the back of the car, where it lay in a huddled heap.

The chauffeur, Fabian, was pawing gingerly at his damaged shoulder. Though painful enough, it had been no worse than a flesh wound, leaving the arm only temporarily numbed and useless. Gradually now the strength was returning to it, though the pain in the shoulder was intense.

'Get in, Fabian!' purred Mr. Ni.

'I can't drive with this hole in my shoulder,' growled the chauffeur sullenly.

'You can and you will,' answered Ni, and the dangerous caressing note had crept again into his soft voice.

Without a word the chauffeur took the driving-seat.

For some moments the stout figure in the heavy fur-collared coat, its smooth brown-yellow face like some fat, evil mask in the dim starlight, stood staring down the hillside towards the distant cliffs and the sweep of sea beyond. Mr. Ni produced a long ivory cigarette-holder, inserted a cigarette, and lit it contentedly. A slow smile crept out upon his face.

'I think,' he said aloud, in very gentle tones, 'that Mr. Trevor Lowe will be sorry — very sorry — that he ever let himself become entangled with my affairs, Fabian. I shall make it my business to see that he regrets it — excessively!'

Fabian did not answer. With a smile, Ni stepped into the rear of the car.

A minute later, travelling without lights, the big car was running down the hillside road, the way it had come.

At Ni's feet the huddled form of White stirred and groaned.

Ni bent down, and from under the seat drew a heavy leather strap. With swift fingers he passed it beneath White's elbows, drawing them together behind his back, and fastened the strap. When the secretary recovered his senses, as apparently soon he would, it would be to find his arms pinioned helplessly behind him. Already the Korean was securing a second strap round his wrists.

Again the prisoner stirred and groaned as the dark car arrived now at the foot of the hill, and swung out into the main road.

7

The Trail of the Killer

'What do you make of it, Mr. Lowe?'

Inspector Richards asked the question in the tones of a hopelessly bewildered man.

Letitia Delmar had recovered consciousness, and had told her story. She had seen a figure in the long gallery, moving away from the big picture on which the characters that Lowe had translated had been daubed — a shadowy, furtive figure, hurrying stealthily. It had turned its head, and she had glimpsed for an instant an Oriental face — and had fainted.

Lowe, Dene, and Inspector Richards were in the library now. The body of Sir Matthew Moncrieff had been borne upstairs, and his distraught ward was being cared for in her room. Again the police had searched the house from cellars to roof — without result. Unless

Letitia Delmar had been the victim of an hallucination and the daubed Japanese characters were the work of a traitor in the house — an utterly unlikely contingency — then the mysterious killer had been in the house all the while during the exhaustive searches that had been made for him, avoiding discovery by some seemingly almost superhuman means; had daringly appeared again, and again vanished as if into thin air!

The mysteries that seemed to be the key-problems of the whole grim affair were the twin riddles of the vanished Japanese tramp-steamer, the *Oki Maru*, and that of the stolen Anglo-Japanese treaty from the Foreign Office. That these two mysteries, seemingly linked together, were in some way directly connected with the evil happenings in this old house on the Welsh cliffs, both Low and Dene were confident. But for the moment they were concentrating upon neither of these major problems, nor upon those additional problems that confronted them, as to who was the mysterious Mr. Ni whom White had been sent to trail, and what part in the mystery was being played by Mademoiselle Julie, of the French Secret Service? For the moment, at least, their wits were pooled in an effort to solve the more immediate riddle of the unseen comings and goings of the unknown killer who had slain Moncrieff, and appeared again to daub that sinister message in Japanese characters in the long gallery.

'It's like black magic, sir.' The police-inspector jerked out the words with angry, helpless bewilderment.

Lowe was standing by the big old fireplace, drawing at his pipe in silent thought. Dene, his face set in grim lines, was pacing the floor restlessly. He halted, taking the scarred bulldog briar from between his teeth to growl:

'Well, White's hanging on to Ni's trail, that's one thing!' They had seen the secretary jump for the luggage-grid of Ni's car. 'With luck, we'll soon know something about Ni, at least. Whoever he is, he's mixed up in this ugly game, I'll swear — '

The Secret Service man broke off abruptly. Lowe had suddenly brought his clenched fist crashing down on the low chimney-piece. Dene stared across at him questioningly, as Lowe jerked the curved pipe from his lips.

'By thunder!'

'What's bitten you?' queried Dene laconically.

'Moncrieff's murderer — how he came and went! Where he is now — '

'I — I don't understand, Mr. Lowe!' began the police-officer, in wondering astonishment. 'Do you mean to say that you can tell us — '

Lowe interrupted him. He had produced his automatic.

'Inspector, take this gun — you may need it!' he rasped grimly. 'Go on to the roof, and I'll drive your man to you!'

Richards took the automatic with bewildered countenance. He seemed about to ask further questions, then he accepted his instructions and vanished from the room. They heard him hurrying up the stairs.

'Hanged if I get you, Lowe!' Dene was surveying the dramatist with puzzled eyes.

Lowe smiled for an instant.

'Come with me, Dene. And bring that scuttle, will you?'

He was pointing to a big brass scuttle piled with logs that stood by the fireplace. Dene betrayed no astonishment he may have felt as he swung it up and followed Lowe into the hall. Already Lowe was striding swiftly up the staircase. In the long gallery he turned right, past the big picture on whose glass the daubed white Japanese characters with their sinister message still stared down at them — weird, fantastic hieroglyphics written by an unknown hand.

He made his way without hesitation to one of the rooms that opened from the far end of the gallery — flung the door open, snapping on the light in the room beyond. Dene followed him in wonderingly.

The room was an unoccupied bed-room, a large apartment, its panelled stone walls bearing witness that this was part of the oldest section of the big house. Opposite the door, beyond the heavy old wooden bedstead, a big stained glass window drummed noisily to the bluster-ing wind that surged against it. Lowe closed the door, and Dene stared round.

'Well?' he jerked out.

Lowe was smiling grimly.

'Can't think why I didn't tumble to it before,' he muttered, half to himself. 'The only possible solution.' He flung out a pointing hand, and Dene, following the direction of Lowe's gesture, saw that his companion was pointing to the big, ancient stone fireplace across the room. 'I noticed that old fireplace during my search. A couple of hundred years old, judging from the style of it. And the thing is, it's the only one of the original old fireplaces left in these rooms along the gallery.'

'Great Scott!' breathed Dene. 'The chimney! They built chimneys for men to climb in those days!' His expression altered. 'But you're on the wrong track, that chimney-opening has been built in, you can see.'

'Partly, yes. But I'll be surprised if we don't find some sort of an opening still left, all the same! I tell you, it's the only solution. The murderer seems to appear from the long gallery — and this room, as

I say, is the only one with the original old fireplace left.'

He was crossing the room on swift, silent feet, and an electric flash-lamp had appeared in his hand. Stepping noiselessly into the big arched fireplace, he stooped down and flashed on the torch. Dene saw him thrust up an arm, heard a faint metallic clang and an ejaculation of satisfaction from Lowe.

'Here we are, Dene! As I thought! This chimney-opening has been built in to keep the rain out, of course, owing to the old-fashioned width of the chimney. But an opening has been left, covered by a hinged flap, in case a fire was ever wanted here. Narrow, but not too narrow for a wiry man to get through pretty easily — '

He was playing the torchlight upwards. Dene, stepping into the big old fireplace beside him, peered up, and saw that, as Lowe had prophesied, beyond the open metal flap that had closed it, the original width of the chimney remained — a great square, blackened shaft vanishing into darkness.

'You're right!' he muttered.

'You can see the old original iron staples set in the wall of the chimney for the old chimney-sweeps to climb up by when they were doing their job. Easy for Moncrieff's murderer, once he'd discovered this, to enter or leave the house at will, gaining the roof by a water-pipe or the ivy on the north side of the house.'

Lowe was speaking in low, matter-of-fact tones. But it was evident from the gleam in his eyes that his satisfaction at having hit upon the solution to the problem was intense. Softly he closed the metal flap.

'The house *is* being watched by Richards' men from the grounds, Dene. No one could have escaped from the roof into the grounds without being seen — unless there's been carelessness. Therefore, Moncrieff's murderer is still hiding somewhere in that chimney-shaft, unless I'm much mistaken. These old chimneys twist and wind all over the place; there must be a dozen stone ledges between here and the roof where he could make himself comfortable while waiting until things are safe for his final getaway.

And there's no hurry for him. When I went up to search the roof, soon after the murder, he must have been up there, but had realised the place was watched outside; so, instead of risking climbing down into the grounds, he slipped back down the chimney-shaft that he used for entering the house to wait his chance. Perhaps it was to scare us that he reappeared in the house and daubed that message, though I don't think he can have realised anyone in the house would be able to read it. All the more startling if we couldn't read it! Perhaps that was his idea.'

He smiled grimly.

'If I'm right, and he's still hiding in the shaft, we've got him like a rat in a trap. Richards is on the roof, and his men are watching the house from the grounds. All we have to do is to smoke the hound out.'

Lowe had turned to a cupboard in the wall, in which he had remembered seeing a pile of old newspapers during his search of the house. He carried an armful to the grate and tossed them in, flinging one or two of the logs that had been brought from the library on to the pile.

'Enough paper there to ignite those logs, Dene. And the newspapers will make plenty of smoke by themselves. We'll just wait a minute to give Richards plenty of time to get up on the roof.'

Dene had stepped back under the wide stone chimney-piece, thrusting back the metal flap, listening. But no sound came down the shaft, except for the mutter of wind from high above.

'If he's still hiding up there it looks as though we've got him all right,' he jerked sardonically.

Lowe pulled out a box of matches, struck one, and tossed it into the inflammable mass of wood and paper. The flames curled into life, ran swiftly right and left, leapt higher, a thickening pillar of smoke sucked up through the chimney-opening in a tortuous whorl.

Dene flung another pile of newspapers into the grate, more logs. The crackle and flutter of the flames filled the room as they drew back from the heat of it, and Lowe swung towards the door.

'Up to the roof!' he rasped grimly. 'He

116

can never get back down here through those flames — '

The blazing mass was a fierce sheet of orange flame. Already the logs were fired, the heavy, coiling smoke pouring upwards, as Lowe and the Secret Service man raced together from the room and along towards the stairs.

The trap-door from the top landing that led out on to the roof was open. The stormy night wind met their faces as they swung on he leads.

'If we've smoked that rat out — ' began Dene fiercely, and broke off.

From somewhere to the right, beyond a high slate ridge of gabled roof, a hoarse shout had come to their ears. They recognised the voice of the police-inspector, Richards; and together Lowe and Dene thundered across the leads. They came round the end of the high roof-ridge, and a startled ejaculation broke from between Dene's shut teeth.

Clinging to a wide chimney-stack, from which a pillar of heavy smoke was pluming, was a shadowy figure, its back towards them — Richards, his head sagging sideways where he stood in a queer, loose attitude, clutching for support at the weather-worn masonry. Even as they caught sight of him his grip relaxed, and he seemed to give way at the knees.

They saw him topple sideways and collapse in the shadow of the great stack, inert.

'My God — '

An electric torch had appeared in Lowe's hand. He flashed it on, and the stabbing beam flooded down upon the crumpled shape of the police-officer. There was a thick ejaculation from Dene, standing at Lowe's side, gun in hand, eyes riveted upon the figure at their feet.

Inspector Richards lay huddled and still. In his right hand the automatic that Lowe had given him was still clutched. And between his shoulder-blades the ornate handle of a jewel-studded knife protruded, driven in almost to the hilt.

Lowe dropped on to one knee, drew out the knife with a swift, clean pull from the blood-soaked shoulders. The knife, he saw, had missed the spine, and was too high to have reached the heart. He thrust a hand inside the inspector's coat, feeling for heart-beats. There was a relief in his face as he glanced up at Dene.

'He's alive!'

The senseless man stirred and groaned.

Dene was staring round the shadowy maze of uneven roofs with dangerous eyes. Somewhere not far away was the man who had struck the inspector down, the man whom they had smoked out like a rat from its hole as a result of Lowe's reasoning. But there was no sign of any moving figure among the shadowy slates and leads.

'But he's up here somewhere!' jerked out the Secret Service man fiercely. 'And we'll get him! We must shut that trap — '

Turning, he raced back to the trap-door, slammed it shut. As he turned again a faint sound from somewhere to his left caught his ears. He sprang for the roof-ridge that sloped up beside him, scrambled to the top, and stared over. A dim, swift figure vanished round a distant parapet as he caught sight of it.

Swinging over the sharp-angled ridge,

Dene slid down the farther side, and raced in pursuit over the flat leads that stretched out before him, thumbing down the safety-catch of his automatic as he ran along a high stone coping, with a sheer drop to the garden beneath if he missed his footing for an instant only, leapt a wide well of darkness between two para-pets and again glimpsed the man he hunted disappearing round a high chimney-stack at the far end of the gable.

The Secret Service man tore in pursuit. Whether or not the fugitive figure, undoubtedly that of the man who had struck down Inspector Richards after being forced from his hiding-place, was the same man as the unknown killer who had slain Sir Matthew Moncrieff it was impossible to know. But Dene had no doubts on that score, and he was deter-mined to get his man at any risk.

Not that the murder of Moncrieff was of professional interest where the King's Spy was concerned — that aspect of the case was Trevor Lowe's. But that the murderer of Moncrieff was implicated in the mystery of the stolen treaty from the

Foreign Office which he was straining every effort to solve Dene was convinced. The two trails ran together.

At the end of the gable he halted in the shadow of the big chimney-stack, staring round with an ugly glimmer in his queer blue eyes. No sign of his man; the fugitive had vanished somewhere in the maze of undulating roof-ridges. He listened, but no sound broke the hush but for the mutter of the wind beating in from the sea.

'Where the devil — '

He slipped across to the nearest slope of slates, climbing noiselessly. Beyond, as he peered over the ridge, a further stretch of flat leads, edged by a narrow stone parapet. Empty! No sign of the elusive fugitive.

From somewhere at the far side of the roofs a sudden shout.

'Hell!' breathed Dene, and dropped to the flat leads, running swiftly in the direction from which the shout seemed to have come.

He was not long in ignorance of the cause of that sudden shout.

Scrambling over another ridge of the uneven old roofs, he caught sight of two figures locked together in a savage embrace — two dark, shadowy figures that reeled and swayed together on the coping at the edge of the leads high above the sheer drop to the path that ran below.

One the figure of Lowe, the other a wiry, cat-like figure, possessed, as Dene saw, of an uncanny strength, or he could never have held his own for a moment with Lowe's muscular frame; but all too vague and shadowy for Dene to make out the face of Lowe's antagonist.

What had happened was obvious enough. Lowe, searching the other side of the roofs, had intercepted the hunted man as Dene had driven him round. And now the two were at grips, their trampling feet echoing noisily across the roofs as they fought and struggled on the narrow parapet, close by the huddled form of the knifed police-officer.

Instinctively Dene had whipped up his gun. But good shot though he was, he dared not pick off the man with whom Lowe fought. Even had a lucky shot knocked out the antagonist, the sudden weight of a dead or senseless man might well have sent Lowe backwards over the lofty brink, to crash to his own doom on the flags far below. Besides Dene wanted to take the man alive.

He swung over the ridge and slid down the farther side. Within a yard or two was the edge of the roof, but he was risking that. Though never for a moment did he doubt Lowe's ability to hang on to his capture, it looked as though that capture were such that it was a two-man job to pin him down.

With the clatter of a loosened slate, Dene's heels struck the leads below. And then, as he regained his balance, leaping towards the struggling figures with glimmering, savage eyes, a hoarse shout broke his lips.

A moment before it had seemed as though Lowe, with one hand locked on his enemy's throat and the other wound round the struggling man like a steel chain, had pinned his man helplessly. But the old stonework of the parapet, worn with long years of storm and rain, cracked beneath the weight of the fighting pair — crumbled away abruptly without warning under their feet; and Dene, with a thrill of horror, saw the interlocked figures of the dramatist and his prisoner reel out over the edge, and fall from sight.

'My God!'

A cold hand seemed to close for an instant about Dene's heart.

That Lowe must be dashed to his death, inevitably, together with the second of those struggling figures, seemed certain.

There was a queer splintering crash in place of the faint, ominous thud that Lowe had dreaded to hear. The Secret Service man sprang to the edge of the roof and stared down.

Directly beneath a great chestnut tree grew close to the wall of the house. He saw the figure of Lowe lying twisted among the bare branches in an ugly way, his shoulders caught in the fork of two thick boughs, his head sagging back loosely. He made no movement. Caught in the branches near him another dark figure was struggling like some great cat. Dene saw the glitter of two eyes that stared up at him for a moment — and then the man had swung along the bough with swift agility, and vanished by the main trunk.

As luck would have it, Lowe had been injured — stunned, and his antagonist had escaped damage in the fall, and was already climbing to earth. Michael Dene crouched with raised gun on the high, broken parapet, peering down.

From somewhere in the grounds he heard a distant shout, followed by the shrill note of a policeman's whistle, the sound of heavy running footsteps approaching below. And then, as the Secret Service man glimpsed the climbing figure in the tree once more — at the same moment that the uniformed figure of one of the police-constables watching the house came racing into view — he pressed the trigger, and the bullet sang down through the gaunt branches.

Despite the interlacing boughs, the bullet found its mark. He heard a faint cry from the shadows, and a figure fell from one of the lower branches to the grass beneath.

The constable had halted a little distance away, staring up in doubt and bewilderment at the crouching figure of Dene on the parapet. He had not noticed the fallen man, nor the twisted figure of Lowe caught amid the upper branches. Already the fallen man was struggling to his feet — evidently Dene's shot had only winged him.

'Get him, you fool!' shouted Dene savagely; and the startled constable, catching sight of his quarry, flung himself forward at the fugitive.

A knife flashed in the starlight; the knife that Lowe had drawn from the inspector's shoulders had not, then, been his only weapon. The glittering blade flew through the air, and with a choking cry the constable staggered, his hand clapped to his neck. The knife had missed his throat, but had slashed deep in passing, and he felt the warm blood flow between his fingers as he clasped the wound dazedly.

The man who had flung the knife was darting away towards the trees across the lawn. Dene whipped up his gun, and the blunt-nosed automatic spoke a second time.

In the half-darkness it was impossible to shoot with any degree of accuracy. The bullet thudded into the turf within an inch or two of the running figure — and then the cat-like form of the fugitive had vanished from sight into the trees.

Dene leapt to his feet and raced back across the starlit leads towards the trap-door by which he and Lowe had gained the roofs. Dragging the heavy trap open, he dropped to the floor below and ran for the stairs.

'What was it? Oh, what was it?' The frightened tones of Letitia Delmar met the Secret Service man as he leapt down the stairs that led from the upper floors to the long gallery.

For an instant he paused.

The pale-faced girl was standing by the head of the lower staircase that ran down to the big hall. She had evidently heard the shots from the roof — had left her room to discover the cause.

Her hand fastened tremblingly upon his arm.

'What was it?' she repeated wildly.

'It's all right,' replied Dene. 'Get back to your room, and don't worry.'

He sprang for the next staircase, racing down into the hall. A few moments later he was in the garden — gun in hand.

He found the constable with the neck wound staggering back along the path, white-faced, his helmet awry. A second constable was appearing on the scene across one of the lawns, and the third, also responding to the whistle and the sound of the shots, could be heard running along the path. Dene gripped the wounded man by the shoulder and rapped out terse orders, then broke into a run for the clump of firs into which the man they had hunted from the roof had vanished.

That Lowe and the two wounded policemen — the inspector, of the two, was infinitely the more badly hurt — would be seen to at once his orders had ensured, and he was taking upon himself the task of following the trail of the murderer of Moncrieff!

He reached the trees and plunged into

their dark shadow; paused, listening.

From somewhere ahead he fancied he heard a faint footfall dying away in the direction of the cliffs.

He broke into a swift swinging run.

Beyond the trees a path led between dark shrubberies to a gate that opened from the grounds of the old house on to a footpath crossing the cliffs. The gate was standing open, and in a patch of mud between the gateposts he saw the imprint of a human foot, deep at the toe — the footprint of a running man.

Reckless of the danger of exposing himself on the open cliffs as a target for a possible bullet, he took the wind-swept footpath towards the cliff-edge.

The sea wind was whipping across the undulating stretches of coarse short grass, the ragged cliff-edge a jagged line ahead against the stormy sea. A maze of wild rocky headlands and cavernous inlets stretched right and left along the shadowy coast, among which shingly paths twisted and climbed tortuously; and Dene realised, as he saw the nature of the stretch of coast on which the old house was situated, the difficulties of the task he had now set himself.

A thousand hiding-places for a fugitive!

He halted at last in the shadow of a great gaunt boulder near the cliff-edge, peering round, tense, alert, straining his ears. Though no track showed on these shingly cliff-paths, the loose stones were noisy under the feet, and he listened hopefully. But no sound of a running man came out of the night.

No sound, no sign! And a maze of shadowy rocks and gullies to hide him.

And then, staring down over the cliff-edge, the Secret Service man gave a low ejaculation, and his teeth clicked together with savage satisfaction.

Riding at anchor in the little cove below, in the dark lee of one of the great flanking headlands, vaguely visible, was a small steam-yacht — riding without lights.

Something significant, sinister, in the fact of the vessel anchored under the cliffs, pitching and rolling to the surge of the foam-capped waves, being there without lights, anxious to avoid notice.

A sardonic smile twisted his lips.

There was a queer, dangerous glimmer in his pale blue eyes as he stared down at the mystery vessel sheltered in the lee of the great headland. Suddenly his fingers tightened on the butt of his gun.

Out from the foot of the cliffs, so far beneath as to seem almost like a toy boat dancing amid the waves, a lean motor-launch — also without lights — had appeared within his range of vision, heading out towards the anchored yacht.

8

On Board the 'Sea Witch'

In the shadow of the great boulder on the cliff-edge the Secret Service man watched the dark launch reel swiftly through the waves towards the vessel at the far side of the little cove. That the launch contained the man he hunted he felt confident, though the launch was too far below for him to distinguish anything recognisable of the two tiny figures that could be seen crouched on board.

Travelling swiftly, the spray high-flung from its lean bows, the launch curved in alongside the bigger vessel and disappeared from view on the farther side. Dene fancied he could make out the shadowy figures of men who had appeared on the yacht's deck. Apparently the launch was being swung inboard on davits.

Who these men were was a mystery;

but it was a mystery that he meant to solve at any cost!

With eager eye he searched the beach below. A dark shape that looked like some kind of a rowing-boat was drawn up on the shingle at the far end of the beach, close under the cliffs — probably a dinghy belonging to the house of Moncrieff. Thrusting his gun back into his pocket, he took the narrow treacherous path that led down to the beach, and little more than a minute later was pounding across the loose shingle under the cliffs towards the little craft drawn up there above the high-water line.

It proved to be a small dinghy, with a pair of sculls lying in it, chained to a thwart. It was the work of moments to smash the padlock that secured them, and with a rattle of shingle the Secret Service man dragged the dinghy down to the water's edge.

There was little chance that those on board the mystery vessel anchored under the headland had seen him; and by keeping to the darkness under the headland, with luck on his side, he would be able, he told himself, to reach the anchored yacht unobserved.

Boarding it would be another matter.

With a powerful thrust, he sent the dinghy shooting out into the breakers, leapt in, drenched with spray and soaked with sea-water to his knees. A curling phosphorus-flecked wave came surging out of the dark, threatening to fling the cockleshell craft back upon the shelving shingle; but already he had the sculls thrust out, and with a fierce pull dragged the dinghy through the foaming crest, out over the next curling breaker to the dark, leaping water beyond. The dinghy was half-flooded, the water washing round his legs — for the first breaker had dumped a mass of black sea-water over the bows — but it still rode buoyantly enough, and Dene was not wasting possibly precious seconds baling.

The wind seemed to be dropping, though the heavy seas were still foaming into the cove with savage fury. Clouds were drifting up over the stars as he pulled steadily across the cove towards the farther headland.

Under the headland the water was quieter. But there was a strong current running, and it needed all his strength to keep the plunging dinghy from being sucked in towards the rocks; jagged, treacherous rocks that rose darkly in the gloom, pierced with echoing caverns where the black water boiled and swirled.

He flung a glance over his shoulder. He was nearer now to the anchored yacht, but still there was a long stretch of difficult water between them. And he heard now a sound that caused his lips to tighten and the muscles of his arms to stand out like knotted rope as he dragged still more fiercely on the oars — the sound of a rattling anchor-chain, and the clatter of a donkey-engine as it hauled the anchor in.

The mystery vessel was getting under way.

The spreading clouds drifting across the sky had made that black shadow in the lee of the headland still more impenetrable — the first time luck had been on his side that night, as he told himself with a hard grin. It would take keen eyes to see him approaching the yacht; and, since those on board were unlikely to be on the lookout for such a visit, the chances were all in his favour — if he could get to it in time.

Lurching and plunging, but drawing nearer yard by yard to the unlighted yacht riding there so furtively, the little dinghy crept on through the darkness.

He was very near now. Peering round, he could make out the name of the yacht, painted on her swaying stern — *Sea Witch*. No one was visible on the little after-deck. But the anchor-chain could still be heard clanking, above the noisy wash of the waves, and suddenly the yacht's single screw woke to life, threshing to foam the water beneath her sharply-cut-away stern. She began to draw slowly forward as the screws quickened and gripped; and Dene, dragging on the oars with all his tremendous strength, was only just in time to catch at the rope-ladder that still hung down her side from the little after-deck, evidently the means by which the men from the launch had got aboard before their little craft had been swung inboard after them. He rose, swinging across the plunging gunwale of the dinghy on to the ladder — and the dinghy fell astern as the yacht drew away towards the mouth of the cove.

A few moments more and he was crouching on the shadowy little deck, peering for'ard, a savage grin on his face as he felt coolly for his gun.

The mad recklessness of his manoeuvre did not worry him. He was single-handed on board this mysterious vessel, bound now, it seemed, for some unknown destination; single-handed against obvious odds, with at least one killer on board. But these things did not weigh against the fact that he was close now on the trail of the man he hunted.

Footsteps rang out suddenly near him. He crouched lower, shifting his grip from the butt to the muzzle of his gun. A dim figure loomed up near the rail, moving towards the ladder. He glimpsed a face that said 'crook,' if ever a face did — swarthy, brutal-mouthed; and then the big figure had caught sight of him, halted in astonishment.

For an instant the two men were

motionless, the look in the astonished eyes of the new arrival on the after-deck changing to startled perturbation. He opened his mouth to shout. But before a sound could come Dene's automatic had crashed down butt-ended on his skull, and his man went down dazedly with a stifled moan.

The next instant he was pinned to the boards, and the hands of the Secret Service man had him round the throat with a grip that brought the fallen giant's tongue protruding between his blackened teeth, as his eyes stared up in terror, white and bulging.

There was an ugly sound as Dene's fist hammered twice on his jaw. The man's struggles ceased abruptly, and he lay spreadeagled without further movement.

'That's your bed-time story,' muttered Michael Dene sardonically, as he rose silently to his feet.

For'ard, past the dark walls of the saloon, ahead of the squat yellow funnel, from which a plume of smoke was being whipped away on the wind, he could see the little navigation bridge, could make out a dark figure there. He heard the tinkle of the bridge telegraph. Otherwise, the dark, unlighted craft was silent but for the hiss of waves against her hull as she crept forward past the end of the great headland and turned for open water.

On noiseless feet, Dene stole forward.

A chink of light was visible through a skylight set in the deck near the doors of the upper saloon; he caught sight of it suddenly as he came abreast of the skylight, and he paused, peering down.

The skylight was open a fraction. It was through the narrow opening that the slit of light streamed — evidently just switched on. The glass itself was covered with a blind beneath. A vaguely audible voice came to his ears from below.

Dropping to his knees, the Secret Service man put his eyes to the narrow opening.

He was looking down into some kind of small saloon, but his range of vision was narrow, and he could see no one. A man's voice rose to him, but the words were indistinguishable, so softly spoken and drowned by the wash of water past the yacht as the *Sea Witch* quickened her speed.

The man's voice was followed by another; and Michael Dene's eyes glimmered strangely as he listened. A woman's voice — and a woman had been the last thing he had expected to find on board this vessel!

Something familiar about that soft, seductive voice, though he could scarcely hear it. He listened, for the moment bewildered by that odd sense of recognition. And then in a flash the truth came to him, and an involuntary exclamation checked in his throat.

'By the Lord Harry!' he breathed.

He had recognised the voice even before a movement of the speaker brought her into his range of vision. A face in the saloon below, full of charm and fascination, youthful and symmetrical, with dark, alluring eyes and wonderful hair like burnished bronze, shining in the soft light like spun silk.

She was smiling, her delicately-rouged lips parted, revealing the whiteness of her teeth; speaking to someone unseen, with a shrug of her slim, silk-clad shoulders, vivacious eyes flashing vividly beneath the pencilled brows.

'Julie!' breathed Michael Dene.

No wonder he had thought from the first moment of hearing it that the girl's voice from below had seemed queerly familiar.

The voice of Mademoiselle Julie — trusted agent of the French Secret Service, he had already known to be as interested as himself in the vanished treaty that the British Government sought to recover at any cost, but whom he had somehow never for an instant dreamed of finding on board this mystery vessel!

'By James — '

Eyes riveted to the narrow slit of the open skylight, he crouched noiseless on the swaying deck, as the *Sea Witch*, rounding the high headland, plunged steeply to the waves. He could not hear what the girl was saying, for the yacht's engines were throbbing louder. But now a second face came into his line of vision, and his jaw clenched.

He had seen that yellow, moon-like face

with the evil, inscrutable eyes not much more than an hour ago, in the house where Sir Matthew Moncrieff had died at the hands of a man whom Dene believed to be now on board this yacht.

Tsu Ni!

'So Julie's in with Ni!'

Ni on board this mystery yacht with Mlle. Julie — what strange undercurrents behind the riddle of the lost Anglo-Japanese treaty and its accompanying mysteries, the vanishing of the *Oki Maru* one night out from Liverpool, and the murder of Moncrieff — what queer trick of Fate had brought these two together?

Pitching and rolling to the heavy seas, the *Sea Witch* was clear of the headland now. Her sidelights and mast-lights were turned on abruptly — as if, clear now of the cove of Moncrieff's house, she no longer bothered to avoid notice. The blustering wind surged across the little after-deck where Dene crouched by the little skylight, ears strained to catch the words spoken in the narrow saloon below.

What had happened to White? he wondered. It seemed probable to the

Secret Service man that he had been thrown off the trail when Ni had joined the waiting yacht — was already back at the house by now, he told himself, to find Lowe temporarily hors de combat.

Ni had vanished now from Dene's range of vision. But the beautiful face of the girl was still visible in the lighted saloon beneath, speaking softly, her alluring dark eyes fastened upon the unseen Oriental.

Her face vanished as she moved away, her slender figure coming into view. And Michael Dene caught his breath — at the same moment that he heard a soft, horrible laugh from the invisible Ni.

For, like a revelation to upset all his new reckonings in a flash, Dene could see now a fact that had previously been hidden from him by the narrowness of his view through the crack of the open skylight.

Mlle. Julie's slender wrists were bound behind her by a tightly-knotted cord.

The girl was a prisoner on board the *Sea Witch*!

9

The Stolen Treaty

Mlle. Julie, standing in the swaying little saloon as the *Sea Witch* pitched through the steep waves beyond the great headland, her lissom figure balanced gracefully to the motion of the vessel, looked across at the gross figure of her captor with coolly smiling eyes.

'And now, monsieur?' she questioned, with a languid shrug of silken shoulders.

She had long ago given up the attempt to free her hands. Her wrists had been bound too well for that to be other than a waste of time. But not for a moment did her casual air of smiling aplomb desert her.

The Korean, a smile of sleepy satisfaction on his round, bland, yellow-brown face, had seated himself in a cushioned chair, extracting a long and slender cigarette holder as he surveyed his lovely captive with a suave smile. He inserted a cigarette in the holder, lit it, blew a thin trail of smoke from his smiling lips to the skylight above, and watched the draught suck the smoke away through the narrow slit of the skylight's opening, before returning his gaze to the beautiful figure opposite him.

'Maintenant, mam'selle?' He spoke in French. Mr. Tsu Ni spoke French as perfectly as English, as perfectly as his own native Korean. 'That is indeed the question!'

He leant forward in his chair. The black eyes fastened upon her were suddenly snake-like, though the fat, yellow face still smiled suavely. There was sheer evil in those eyes, but there was no trace of fear in the eyes of Mlle. Julie — only a coolly mocking gleam, though she knew her danger.

'You and I, mademoiselle, are working upon the same business!' said Ni, in his most dangerously caressing voice. 'We cannot both win. And I do not intend to allow competition. It is necessary for me to end as the winner!'

'C'est ça?' she mocked coolly.

'Mais oui, mam'selle!' He leant back in his chair, a figure of stout complacency. 'I repeat, we cannot both win. And since it happens that you have fallen into my hands — '

He shrugged his massive shoulders. Never for a moment did his eyes leave the lovely face of the French girl. Again he blew a thin stream of cigarette smoke to the skylight, watching it vanish through the narrow opening above.

'There will be no further competition between us!' he continued softly. 'Because, my dear young lady, you will not return from this little sea trip! It distresses me. But as soon as we are well out from the shore, mam'selle, it will be my painful task to send you to a watery grave.' He laughed gently. 'The French Secret Service will be most distressed at the mysterious disappearance of their most beautiful and skilful agent — n'est ce pas?'

Again he shrugged his stout shoulders.

'Alas! the liability to disappear mysteriously at any time is the penalty of your reckless profession, mam'selle. The Secret

Service pays its people well. But hanging over each and every one of you is ever the shadow of death — death, unseen, mysterious, unaccountable. You cannot complain, therefore. You must know, of course, these dangers of your work.'

Mademoiselle Julie smiled, entirely self-possessed.

'But of course, monsieur. It is the penalty of the game. But I have many lives, mon ami — '

'But there are also many ways of dying!' murmured Ni softly. 'Mam'selle — '

The suave words went unfinished.

A sudden sound from above caused Ni to glance upwards, and he saw that one window of the skylight was opening. He saw a shadowy face with pale, glimmering eyes staring down at him, and his lips opened soundlessly. As he started to his feet, a man's figure came swinging down through the opening, dropped to the floor below with lithe strength, and stood surveying him silently, one hand in his pocket; and through the cloth an ominous bulge was visible, the outlined nose of a gun.

There was a twisted smile on Dene's face as his eyes shifted from Ni to the amazed French girl. Ni was on his feet now, clutching the narrow, clamped-down table before him, eyes ablaze.

For some moments there was an electric silence, except for the wash of waves audible through the open skylight. The little saloon swayed heavily, Dene balancing himself to the motion with easy panther-grace.

'Well, Julie? Not seen you for a long time! How's things?'

There was a note of sardonic amusement in the deep voice.

'Monsieur Dene!' The melodious voice was spell-bound.

Mlle. Julie seldom betrayed such sheer astonishment as was visible in her face now. She caught her breath wonderingly. Then her face broke into a whimsical smile. She laughed, very softly, her fascinating eyes dancing.

'So! You, too, m'sieur, are competing in this affair? Eh bien! A three-cornered fight! How in the world you come to be here on board this boat, I wonder, m'sieur? But — cela! — I will not ask!'

'Then I won't ask how you fell into his hands!' grinned Michael Dene.

His eyes had swung back to the stout, half-crouching figure of Ni. Before the warning shift of Dene's finger to the trigger, Mr. Ni slowly raised his arms above his head.

He had recovered his composure in amazing fashion.

A moment before his eyes had been blazing with malignant bewilderment and fury, the lips drawn back, the smooth, yellow-brown face strangely contorted. Now he was bland and smiling, seemingly perfectly at his ease, as he stood with a suave, almost mocking smile upon his face, surveying Dene without a trace of perturbation or even surprise.

'So unexpected, I confess, your — er — arrival!' murmured the Korean blandly. 'I recognise you, I believe, as one of the police officers at Mr. Moncrieff's house? Where is Mr. Trevor Lowe?'

'You recognised Lowe, then?'

The Korean inclined his sleek head — the black hair so heavily oiled as to gleam like polished jet.

'Well, I'm no police officer!' rasped Dene sardonically. 'Never mind who I am, Ni! No, don't slide towards that bell. I should hate your men to find you lying here with your brains blown all over the floor. I shouldn't shout, either. That would be a fatal mistake, believe me!'

Stepping forward, he thrust the nose of his automatic into the fleshy chest of the Korean, and with his free hand ran expert fingers over the stout figure. He pulled a small gun from Ni's waistcoat — there was a neat holster sewn inside the loose waistcoat, under the left armpit — and dropped the weapon into his own pocket.

'No knives, then, Ni? Used 'em all up at Moncrieff's house — eh? Or perhaps that was one of your pals?'

'I fail to understand,' murmured Ni blandly.

He had lowered his hands in response to a gesture of permission from the Secret Service man.

'I wonder!' returned Dene laconically. 'Untie that girl's hands, Ni!'

Mlle. Julie turned so that her back was

turned towards Dene. The girl knew all the tricks of the game, and she was not giving Ni the chance of stepping behind her to untie her hands, then holding her as a shield while he shouted for aid. Ni crossed towards her, and with calm, unhurried fingers untied the knots. Julie stretched her freed arms with a little wry grimace.

'That is a great deal better,' she said quietly. 'Merci, m'sieur!'

'I take it that if you were armed, earlier on, they've taken your gun from you,' remarked Dene, with a smile. 'So I needn't search you, Julie!'

'You do not trust me?' She asked the question with an air of charming reproach.

Dene grinned.

'Not an inch!' he responded cheerfully. 'As you know thundering well, my dear! You're after that stolen treaty or I'm a Dutchman — unless you've got it already! And I'm out to queer your game, I'll tell you — '

'The — the stolen treaty?' Her pretty forehead puckered as if in bewilderment.

Again Dene grinned.

'Don't try that bluff, Julie! It won't wash! Still, I fancy you haven't got your pretty fingers on it yet awhile, and for the moment at least you and I seem both to be in the same boat — in more ways than one!' he added, with sardonic humour. 'We'd better call a truce until we're safe back on shore, ma'm'selle — if we ever do get back!' He swung towards Ni. The gun in his hand had never for an instant shifted from covering the Korean's heart. 'As for you — I want a talk with you, Ni! You're going to tell me things — '

'I have nothing to tell,' came the bland answer. 'I fail to understand — '

'Like blazes you fail to understand!' muttered Dene.

He broke off as footsteps sounded on the deck above, and, with a menacing tilt of his gun, he warned the Korean to silence. The footsteps died away. Evidently the man on deck had failed to notice a certain gagged and bound figure lying hidden in the black shadow of the upper saloon. Dene had taken care that the man he had knocked out on boarding

152

the *Sea Witch* should not recover his senses and raise the alarm before he had dropped into the saloon below.

'Never heard of the *Oki Maru* — eh, Ni?'

It was a sighting-shot on Dene's part, but it registered a hit, for the Korean's eyes seemed to flicker for a split second in a way that told the Secret Service man that Mr. Tsu Ni was by no means ignorant concerning the vanished Japanese steamer.

'I see you have. You'll have heard, too, of a certain clever robbery from a Foreign Office safe that happened some little while ago? Eh, Ni?'

Ni did not answer.

Dene glanced curiously at Mlle. Julie, Ni watching them as a snake watches a mouse.

'I wonder just how much you know, Julie?' he muttered reflectively, and was met with an innocent, disarming smile.

'Not talking, eh, Julie? They say women are talkative, but they can't have met you!' he grinned approvingly.

The *Sea Witch* was steaming along in a

leisurely way, travelling at an easy ten knots or so. The wind seemed to be dying down considerably. A tense silence filled the night — only the throb of the yacht's engines and the vague hiss of waves.

Ni knocked the half-smoked cigarette from his long holder and, carefully inserting another, lit it smilingly.

'Mr. Dene, I admire your bravery in coming aboard my yacht in this somewhat reckless fashion. But how do you imagine you can leave it? If you care to attempt to swim to shore — both you and the lady — I shall be charmed to bid you adieu! I am afraid, however, that such a swim would be suicidal to attempt, as we are already a considerable distance from the coast. One has, therefore, to come to the conclusion that, although at the moment you have control of me personally, thanks to that weapon in your hand, nevertheless you are my prisoner! Both you and the lady! Before long your presence on board is bound to be discovered. What then?'

The suave words were spoken with a soft caressiveness that was infinitely more sinister than any gloating triumph could have been. The man reminded Dene of a fat mamba — that deadly African snake that has only to strike once, if it strikes truly, for death to follow within seconds.

'You think you've got us, Ni?' His grin was not pretty to look at. 'I think not! You're going to give orders to the skipper of this yacht of yours — my orders! And while you give them there'll be something nosing round your spine that would be the last thing you'd feel on earth if you didn't do as you were told. This!'

He tapped his gun.

'But first, as I've said, you're going to tell me things! Where's that stolen treaty, Ni? Have you got it — or has someone else? Someone else, I suppose, or you wouldn't have had to worry about this girl here interfering with your hunt for it! But you know where it is, I'll swear — and, by thunder, you're going to tell me within — what shall we say? — thirty seconds! Yes, thirty seconds. And I'll know if you're lying! No man fools me with a lie, I warn you! I'm not that easy!'

He had taken a watch from his pocket

and laid it on the table. The tiny second-hand was circling briskly.

'Keep track of those seconds, Julie!'

The girl stepped quickly to the table, and her eagerness brought a slow smile to Dene's lips. He chuckled softly.

'Not often I have the pleasure of tricking anything out of you, Julie! Thanks a lot! Evidently you don't know where the treaty is, or you wouldn't have been so keen to hear what Ni has to say, would you? But you want to know badly!'

For a second the girl seemed disconcerted, and few men had ever seen Mlle. Julie disconcerted even for that brief moment of time. Then she laughed, coolly enough.

'You are a clever man, M'sieur Dene — n'est-ce-pas?'

'Sure!' agreed Michael Dene dryly. His eyes fastened upon Ni, hard, relentless. 'Spill it, Ni!'

The snake-like eyes of the Korean stared back at him inscrutably. Ni was silent, blandly unconcerned — outwardly, at least.

'If you value your health, you'll answer

my question, Ni! I don't know where this craft of yours is bound for, but by thunder — '

A sudden hoarse shout from somewhere above broke in upon Dene's fiercely-muttered words.

They heard running feet on the after-deck above their heads; another startled shout —

'Hell take the luck!' murmured Dene coolly.

For he knew that the bound man on the deck above had been discovered, and that soon a hornets' nest would break around their ears.

Mlle. Julie was listening to the excited sounds above with as much coolness as Dene himself. She climbed swiftly on to the table in the narrow, swaying saloon, and slammed shut the open skylight, driving home the bolt that fastened it.

'Now for what you English call a 'rough house,' is it not?' she said, with a quiet little smile. 'I could not have a better — friend for the 'rough house,'' she added softly, and her eyes danced alluringly as they met his.

'Listen, Julie! We're together in this. No funny business! We're together — till we get ashore — if ever we do, alive!'

She nodded, and though they were fundamental enemies in this grim affair of the stolen treaty, despite the fact that fate had flung them together now, Dene knew that he could trust the girl to keep her word. He snatched Ni's gun from his pocket and thrust it into her hands.

'Better take this!'

She took the gun in a way that showed how well used her pretty hand was to handling such a weapon.

Above their heads the excited sounds were dying away already. Hurrying footsteps were lost to their ears along the deck. Soon Ni's men would be coming to tell their chief of their discovery, and if the bound man had recovered his senses by now, to tell the reason of it.

Ni had seated his stout frame comfortably in one of the cabin chairs. His round, yellow face was inexpressibly bland, his voice sinister with caressiveness.

'Now, my charming friends!' He smiled, and carelessly flicked the ash from his cigarette with a manicured yellow finger.

With a swift stride, Michael Dene was across the narrow saloon; his knotted fingers took Ni by the throat, whilst his gun rammed hard and savage into the stout man's teeth. Ni gave a swift, convulsive struggle, then froze still at the menace of that cold steel rim thrust between his lips. His eyes stared up into Dene's — black, malignant.

'Quick, man!' rasped the Secret Service man, and his voice was harsh with grim purpose. 'Tell me, damn you! If you've not got it, who has — that stolen treaty? You're on its trail — you know! Where is it, Ni?'

In his heart he never believed the bluff would work, for it was clear that he needed Ni alive. Ni, too, realised that fact — but a shadow of a second too late!

'On the *Oki Maru!*'

The choked words broke in terror from his lips; and then he realised — too late — that he had fallen for a bluff, and the yellow face went baleful with chagrin.

Dene stepped back, with a hard laugh.

159

'Thanks, Ni! And I take it you don't know where the *Oki Maru* is, or you would have had the treaty by now. A mystery where she vanished, too! But we're level now, at least.'

Already he was wondering — what was the mysterious connection between the *Oki Maru* and the big house on the cliffs where Moncrieff had died at a killer's hands? But there was no time to voice the thought. Running feet could be heard approaching the door of the saloon.

Mlle. Julie was standing by the door; her slim fingers had just turned the key in the lock.

Whether she had heard Ni's momentarily terror-stricken admission Dene could not tell. The girl's eyes were fastened on the locked door, and the gun in her hand was half-raised.

The handle turned and rattled. There was a loud knock on the panels, a shout from the alleyway.

Ni had staggered to his feet, his face working strangely. Dene gripped him by the shoulder, and his gun implanted a cold kiss upon the fleshy yellow neck.

'You can open that door now, Julie!' he rasped.

The girl turned the key in the lock and flung the narrow door wide, stepping back towards the wall, her gleaming weapon levelled and steady.

Four men were crowded in the alleyway outside, three white men and an Oriental; a Korean, as Dene guessed. One of the white men he recognised, apart from the swollen, bruised jaw, as the lusty giant he had 'outed' on boarding the *Sea Witch*.

The four men stared into the saloon with startled bewilderment, dumb. Dene shifted his grip on Ni to the stout Korean's collar. The nose of his automatic, however, did not shift an inch from where it pressed hard into Ni's neck.

'Come right in, gentlemen!' he said with a smile.

10

Turned Back!

There was no response to Michael Dene's sardonic invitation.

The four men crowded together in the narrow doorway, staring in with bewildered faces, had read the danger-light in the queer glimmering eyes of the big figure who held their master in a steel grip, with a gun at his neck. They remained where they were, their eyes shifting in dumb bewilderment from the Secret Service man to the silk-clad, graceful girl who covered them so coolly, a slight smile playing on her delicately-rouged lips.

A tense, waiting silence, broken at last by a savage, startled oath from the man with the bruised jaw as he recognised Dene as the mysterious attacker who had knocked him senseless on the deck above.

'That's him!' he panted.

The man with the purpled jaw was glaring across at Dene, with evil fury in his bloodshot eyes. His leg-of-mutton hand rose to his damaged face as he took a sudden, lurching step forward, then halted, his eyes shifting back swiftly to Julie's poised, languorous figure, with its significantly-levelled gun.

'You'll notice the lady has you covered, gentlemen!' murmured Dene, in a tone of grim amusement. 'I'll warn you that she is as expert with a gun as myself. Not that, in any case, it would need a very expert shot for the small task of blowing Mr. Ni's head off his shoulders — which is what I shall do if any of you gentlemen pass that table!'

The smiling, almost bantering tone changed abruptly.

'Understand that, you dock-rats! I'm master of this vessel — unless you prefer to see Ni's neck smashed into a pulp! Get that into your heads!'

Ni began to speak swiftly in his own tongue, his eyes fastened on the yellow man in the doorway with the other three — a small, round-headed, cat-like figure.

But Dene interrupted Ni with a jerk on the man's collar that choked the words back in his throat.

'Talk English while you're with me, you hound!'

He was allowing no secret instructions to be passed between Ni and his yellow satellite. He squeezed the circle of steel harder into the fleshy throat.

'Listen, Ni! You'll be getting a sore throat — and badly — if you don't do as you're told! Tell these wharf-thieves of yours to do as I say if you value your skin as much as I guess you do!'

Ni stared up into the ominous eyes of the big-boned figure that held him, diabolical fury twisting his lips.

Mlle. Julie, watching the four ruffians in the doorway — the yellow man had slipped a step or two into the room, beside the man with the purpled jaw — laughed softly as she balanced her lissom figure lithely to the roll of the yacht, one hand resting carelessly on her silken hip.

'Mes amis,' she muttered softly, 'it will be wise of you all to raise your hands above your heads! Merci, messieurs!' she mocked, as the four hastily obeyed. 'That is much better!'

Keeping the chill circle of steel pressed in Ni's neck, Dene reached out to one of the curtained portholes, dragged the curtain back, peering out into the darkness.

The dark, jagged coastline, backed by the black mountains, was visible away to lee of the *Sea Witch*. The yacht was steaming along swiftly now, her slender bows smashing into the waves with a surging hiss that was audible to their ears.

'Now then, Ni — '

'Well!' snarled Ni malignantly.

'This yacht's turning!' said Dene. 'She's turning back, Ni — right back to where she came from! Send one of these rough-necks to tell 'em so on the bridge. He can tell 'em that unless we make that turn within three minutes, you'll not only be dead but unrecognisable.'

Ni began to stammer a thick-spoken order. Dene interrupted him.

'Never mind talking! I'll do all the talking necessary!'

He turned his glance towards the four

crooks across the saloon. Still utterly bewildered though they evidently were at finding this masterful unknown man with their master in his power, they were beginning to size up the situation now. They were men used to living by their wits — scum of the European port at which Ni had picked them up to man his yacht — men used to living in constant danger of gun and knife; even the steadily levelled weapon in the slim white hand of Mlle. Julie could not cow them for long, closely covered though they realised they were. All together they were edging forward when a contemptuous exclamation from Mlle. Julie checked them.

'You are fools! You think that perhaps one quick rush — Because I am a woman, perhaps I cannot shoot!' She laughed merrily. 'At five hundred yards — not simply five — I could shoot any man of you dead if I liked.'

There was something in her tone that lent conviction to her amused, contemptuous words. The four froze still again, and one who had been about to half-lower his arms thought better of it. Dene chuckled.

'That's better, you poor fools! Thought maybe I didn't mean it, when I said I'd press this trigger? Think again. Just try to rush me! Try it — if you like! You think not, after all! You're wise!'

He fastened his eyes on the big man with the bruised jaw, who muttered evilly as he glared back, his muscular arms raised above his tremendous shoulders.

'You'll do! Trot along to the bridge, and give 'em my message, with my compliments. Tell 'em what I said, that this yacht is to turn back and drop her hook where she came from — if they value Ni's life at the price of half an ounce of lead! You others stand where you are, if you want to keep healthy.'

For a moment or two the big ruffian hesitated. His eyes went to his master.

'Go!' snarled Ni. 'Tell them to turn back!'

Without a word the man swung on his heel and strode from the saloon. The little yellow scoundrel looked for an instant as though he contemplated darting after him. Mlle. Julie shifted her weapon a fraction to cover him, and he saw the significant movement, and remained where he was.

'That is wise, mon ami!' murmured the girl spy.

She crossed to the door, closed it, and stood with her graceful figure between it and the three baffled ruffians. They recoiled from her — they had recognised now that, despite her appearance of charming femininity, this beautiful girl with the cool dark eyes was dangerous!

With a powerful thrust, Dene sent Ni sprawling backwards into a chair. The Korean lay panting, eyes narrowed with hate, hands clenched on the wooden arms.

'Stay there, you stuffed shirt!' drawled the Secret Service man. 'Look after him, Julie! I'll just take an inventory of these scum!'

'Keep your hands off me!' snarled one of the three ruffians as he turned towards him, while Mlle. Julie covered Ni.

'Open your face at me again, and I'll smash it!' rasped Dene fiercely.

He ran swift, searching hands over the trio. Neither of the white men — typical dock-rats both, lean, evil — had a weapon. It occurred to Dene, with a grim smile, that in all likelihood Mr. Tsu Ni, knowing the type of men he employed to run his yacht, took care that they went unarmed other than at times when he required the contrary. But there was a knife under the little Oriental's loose blue jacket — an ugly wisp of steel with the point of a needle. He pocketed it, eyeing the yellow man with thoughtful eyes.

'Wonder if you're the lad who killed Moncrieff?' he rasped.

The man stared at him inscrutably.

'Do you write Japanese?' demanded Dene.

Still the man did not speak.

'Your middle name's Oyster, is it? Whether you speak English or not, I'd take a small bet that you were in that house up on the cliffs there, tonight!' muttered Dene.

But whether or not the silent, cat-like little Korean was the fugitive whom he and Lowe had hunted from the roofs of the old house on the cliffs, did not greatly worry the Secret Service man. If so, the

169

man had served his purpose, so far as Dene was concerned, by leading him to the bigger game.

Moncrieff's murder interested him only as far as it was connected with the matter on which he was working — that of the stolen Anglo-Japanese treaty. It was no part of his business as a Foreign Office agent to get Moncrieff's murderer — that was a thing he was quite willing to leave to Lowe, unless it looked like helping him in his own affairs. Of the four men in the little saloon of the *Sea Witch* just then, it was Ni who interested Dene, for Ni was not only definitely cognisant, as he knew now, of many things he wished to know himself in connection with that mysterious affair, but was evidently working to get his own hands upon the missing document from Whitehall.

Again it flashed into his mind to wonder what had happened to Arnold White, whom he and Lowe had last seen swarming on to the luggage-grid of Ni's car; to wonder, too, if Lowe had been badly hurt, in that fall from the roof when the fugitive they were hunting had been so amazingly fortunate.

He jerked his head towards the far end of the saloon.

'Get over there, you three!' he ordered crisply, and the little Korean and his two white companions sullenly retreated to the end of the saloon, where they and Ni could be kept covered in a bunch. He seated himself on the narrow table, gun cocked on one knee. 'All right, Julie. I'll take care of these prizewinners.'

Ni had recovered some of his smooth suavity now. Whatever his inward feelings, he was veiling them with a calm blandness that Dene — himself an expert in the art of coolness when his back was to the wall — could grimly approve.

'I don't know how much you know, Ni,' he said drawlingly, 'but you're going to spill the whole story some time in the next twelve hours! You're caught! Oh, I'll get you ashore all right — unless I have to shoot you because your men are fools enough to get funny, which I don't imagine they will. Yes, we're turning already, you'll notice — '

Through the uncurtained port-hole he

could see the dim, dark coastline swinging away, as the *Sea Witch*, already slowed, turned her plunging bows.

Those on the bridge had evidently decided to obey! He smiled quietly. Ni watched him; and in his snakelike eyes there was the look of a cornered beast.

But his voice, when he spoke, was steady.

'And how do you propose to get me ashore, my friend?' he murmured.

'Easy!' grinned Dene. 'They'll be searching around those cliffs for me, Ni, and a signal flashed with an electric torch through that porthole will bring 'em out to the yacht. Your crowd, of course, will make a get-away in the launch — except for these three! Let 'em! You're the man I want. And you're the man I've got!'

'I see.' Ni's eyes glittered queerly. 'You are very confident!'

'Sure!' nodded Dene laconically. 'We're headed back for the cove right now!'

Mlle. Julie was lighting a silk-tipped French cigarette that she had extracted from a tiny gold cigarette-case. Her eyes were fastened on Dene as she let a cloud of smoke break gently from her smiling lips.

'And I, m'sieur?' she murmured.

'You'll draw blank!' Dene told her dryly. 'Ni is my meat — Madame D'Elange!'

He saw her start, almost imperceptibly, at his use of the name by which he knew her to have bought the house on the cliffs.

'I've been wondering a lot why you bought that house, Julie!' he went on. 'You know a lot, like Ni — and one thing you seem to share with him is an idea that Moncrieff's house is mixed up in this business. I don't suppose you're on a wrong trail, either, my dear — you seldom are, if ever!'

'Merci, m'sieur!' she said, half mockingly.

'I won't ask you why you think that house is so important,' Dene added with a grim smile. 'For one thing, you wouldn't tell me. And for another, I shall get that out of Ni before I've done — I promise you that!'

She smiled enigmatically. In the soft light of the yacht's saloon, her burnished hair shone like flame, the light playing fantastic tricks amid its gleaming coils. A lovely creature, he told himself — and dangerous! Although for the moment they were allies, they were rivals for the lost treaty, Dene knew; and he knew only too well that Julie, with her alluring beauty and nimble wits, her cool resourcefulness and reckless daring, was a rival more to be feared than most men.

How she had come to fall into Ni's hands was a riddle that he was not bothering about, since she had offered no explanation. Julie must have made a slip for once; unless it were that she had been playing some deep game that as yet he did not understand. Even that was likely — with Julie!

The motion of the yacht had changed, as she steamed now with the waves; an uneasy figure-eight roll had set in. In the saloon silence — but for the murmur of the yacht's engines and the constant hiss of the water, both so regular that the ear forgot them.

Behind the chair in which Ni sat with his oblique black eyes riveted upon Dene, the two white men and the second Korean stood against the white-painted panelling and glared balefully. With half the length of the saloon between them, they dared not make a rush — particularly since the girl by Dene's side also toyed with a watchful automatic; and, so far at least, there was no sign from those on deck. To all appearances — though Dene was not, inwardly, letting himself be too optimistic — those in charge of the yacht were knuckling under to necessity and obeying instructions.

But he was keeping one eye on the door. If an attempt was made to rob him of his present mastery, he was ready to meet it! He had not forgotten the skylight; but that could not be opened from outside. All the trumps were in his hand, he told himself with sardonic satisfaction. As for Julie — she had agreed to their temporary truce, and would keep her word.

Crash!

A rain of splintered glass came smashing down into the saloon from the skylight as something heavy tore through the blind that had covered it and thudded to the floor — a bar of iron, flung against the glass from the deck above.

In a second Dene was off the table, pressed against the far panelling — without his gun, for a moment forgetting its task of covering Ni and his three satellites. Something streaked down through the shattered skylight — a long knife that embedded its point in the table-top where he had been an instant before.

Like a flash Ni was on his feet, his bulky frame poised to leap, and the three behind him started forward at the same second. But they recoiled as they realised that Dene's squat automatic still stared across at them, rock steady. There was an echoing shot; and Mlle. Julie, the gun smoking in her hand as she stood pressed back like Dene against the panelling, laughed coolly. The yellow face that she had glimpsed peering down from above had vanished hastily into the darkness as her bullet ripped out through the broken skylight.

'Clumsy fools!' she exclaimed scornfully. 'They are not quick enough!'

She shrugged and smiled.

Where they stood by the saloon wall they were out of view from above. Dene chuckled deeply.

'You can sit down again, Ni,' he drawled. 'The fun's over. That knife-sharp up there registered a miss, you'll have noticed.'

The look in Ni's face as he dropped back into his seat, breathing queerly, was devilish. From the deck above, through the broken light, they could hear muttering voices as the *Sea Witch* reeled on through the overtaking waves.

'Another fool trick like that one, and you're dead, Ni! You can tell 'em so right now.'

There was a look in the eyes of the Secret Service man that compelled obedience. Ni shouted a thick command, and the vague muttering on the deck ceased. They heard furtive movements — then silence.

Through the smashed skylight the night wind, laden with the tang of the sea, beat down lustily into the little saloon as the *Sea Witch* steamed landwards. On the table-top the long knife quivered like a silver blade to the swaying of the yacht.

'Fond of knives, you Koreans,' remarked Dene dryly. 'It's a dirty game, though, Ni. A gun's clean by comparison — '

His words went unfinished.

A reverberating shock echoed through the lighted saloon, and the floor beneath their feet heeled up as though a giant shoulder had thrust at it. A grinding, dragging crash, that finished with a hideous scrunching of torn steel, and the *Sea Witch* shuddered like a wounded live thing, and came to rest with a lurch that flung the four men and the girl in the narrow, steep-tilted saloon against the far panelling.

Michael Dene, tossed helplessly sideways, felt the gun knocked from his hand against the clamped-down table, crashed heavily against the sloping wall within a yard of the sprawled figure of Ni. His head struck the brass-bound rim of one of the port-holes, and for the moment darkness flooded his brain as he sagged into the angle of floor and wall, semi-stunned.

178

The *Sea Witch* had struck the submerged rocks! The single unforeseen factor to smash his plans.

His head ached sickeningly as he shook the daze from his brain.

Down through the broken skylight, at a steep angle now, a spatter of spray came tossing into the saloon, and the dull concussion of the waves boomed ominously against the hull of the stricken yacht. Shouts and stumbling feet on the deck above — the grinding of steel plates.

Julie was lying near him, dazed for the present by the violence of the shock that had flung her, with the others, the whole width of the saloon. He took a step towards her — difficult to stand on the steeply sloping floor — and then something crashed down upon Dene's head from behind, and the Secret Service man went down like a fallen oak, all consciousness blotted out.

There was an exultant smile on the face of the man who had struck him — Ni himself, standing like some yellow beast with his fleshy fingers tight around the iron bar that had been flung through the skylight by his henchman on the deck above.

Mlle. Julie, struggling to her feet, made a swift, lithe dart for her fallen gun. But Ni, nearer to the weapon than the girl, pounced with that strange agility of which his stout frame was capable, gripped her by a silken shoulder, and flung her back with a tangled Korean oath. As she struggled up again on the sloping floor she saw that the gun was now in Ni's hands where he stood astride the inert figure of Michael Dene — cool, bland, smiling, once more seemingly imperturbable. His three satellites were scrambling across the tilted boards towards the door, wild consternation in their faces; but an order from their master, soft, yet compelling, halted them.

'Cowards!' said Ni steadily. 'Stay where you are!'

Against the hull of the *Sea Witch* the waves were beating heavily, and spray came flinging in through the shattered skylight from the deck. But the yacht was motionless, caught fast on the unseen rocks that had trapped her as in a vice.

No immediate danger, Ni could feel confident, for he knew the tide was falling; not till it rose again, and the *Sea Witch* was lifted from the rocks on which she was embedded, and the sea poured in through her shattered plates, was she likely to slide back into the depths.

His men halted, uncertain, clinging to any support that offered itself. The French girl, facing Ni's menacing gun, shrugged coolly, and slowly raised her arms.

'So, after all, I win!' murmured Ni caressingly.

11

The Clue in Japanese

Michael Dene's first realisation, as his senses came back to him, was of being in some small, tossing vessel that had approached close inshore. His second, that he was bound both hand and foot; and memory came back to him with a rush.

He was lying in the bows of the launch that he had seen from the cliffs go out to the *Sea Witch* in the cove near Moncrieff's house. As the launch pitched steeply to the waves, lifting the bows high, he could see through the murk the vague, dark shape of the yacht, careened on the far-out rocks that were now appearing from the water with the ebbing tide.

That the wreck of the *Sea Witch* had been chance alone he felt convinced. Evidently the men on the bridge had not known these treacherous, rock-infested waters. But had their action been deliberate, it could not have saved Ni more effectively from Dene's mastery of the situation — even at the loss of his yacht.

The launch's engines were beating rhythmically in his ears, the hiss of foaming water rising and falling by his head. The dull ache in his head bore witness to the force with which he had been struck down. But with an effort he cleared his senses, and out of the gloom the bland face of Mr. Ni appeared, smiling down at him. Other vague figures —

'I am afraid, Mr. Dene, that your chivalry was unfortunate — for you.' The soft, evil voice was mocking. 'You were, for the moment, too concerned for the lady to notice your own dangers, were you not? How chivalrous — and how singularly unfortunate for both of you!'

'Cut it out!' begged Dene impatiently. 'What's next, Ni?'

His aching eyes made out now more clearly the figures crowded in the stern of the launch. With a start, he saw that Julie was among them, sitting with her slender wrists bound behind her, looking across at him with a queer little smile.

'I am sorry, m'sieur!' she said quietly. 'But for me perhaps — '

Dene grinned crookedly where he lay.

'Nonsense, Julie,' he said brusquely. 'Well, Ni?' Again he fastened curious eyes upon the complacent figure of their captor.

'I have decided, for the moment, to allow you to live,' came the purring answer.

'Kind of you,' drawled Dene.

'Not in the least, my dear sir. You see, had I killed you both on the yacht, and thrown your bodies overboard, they would inevitably have been washed up much sooner than I should have wished. Even to have weighted them would not have been a certain way of preventing that. And I have no wish for your bodies to be found — yet awhile. On the other hand, to have brought you ashore dead would have been even more troublesome than bringing you ashore alive — a dead man is a heavy, cumbersome article — '

'Sure!' said Dene. 'And I should just have hated to give you that trouble.'

'Wherefore,' continued Ni blandly, with a gesture of his fleshy hands, 'you still live. I do not say that you will continue to live for very long.'

'That's right,' agreed Dene dryly. 'Don't say anything rash, Ni.'

'You are not, then, afraid to die?'

The other laughed.

'Afraid? Well — I'm not dead yet!'

'You are a brave man, Mr. Dene,' murmured Ni smilingly. 'You can laugh in the face of death, as a man should.'

'You can miss out the bouquets,' Dene told him sardonically. 'And listen, you fat mamba, you're going to let that girl go! Understand?'

'I am afraid, Mr. Dene, you are no longer in the position to give orders,' the Korean answered, with evil gentleness. 'So unfortunate, is it not?'

His teeth showed white in the faint light, as his lips curled back.

The launch slipped in past a high headland, and the distant yacht was blotted from view. Dene lay silent. Talk was useless — but he was thinking hard.

He and Julie were in a tight corner; no good shutting one's eyes to that. But he told himself that he had been in tight corners before — and yet still lived.

There were four men with Julie in the stern of the launch. Not all the yacht's crew by a long way, so presumably the launch would be returning for the others, or they had taken to the other boats — which seemed more likely. Securely though the *Sea Witch* was apparently held, her weight as the tide fell might cause her to swing over and go down at any time, even though most probably she would remain till the next tide rose and took her.

Not for the first time in his life, Dene was having cause to admire Julie's cool self-assurance in the face of sinister dangers. He could see that she was as calmly self-possessed, despite this ugly turning of the tables, as when, gun in hand, she had been covering Ni's satellites in the *Sea Witch*.

'No rattling her,' he told himself appraisingly.

Though the ache in his head still made

clear thinking difficult, his brain was growing gradually clearer. The launch was heading for a tiny shingly beach between two converging walls of cliff, as he soon saw; and wondered how far they were from the house where he had left Trevor Lowe.

The nose of the launch took the shingle with a grinding crunch in the black shadow of the cliffs that towered on either side. A winding path led up from the beach, and a few minutes later he and Julie, their arms still bound, guns behind them, were being hustled up the steep ascent by Ni's men, with Ni following, a cigarette glowing in his long holder. The wash of waves on the shingle below rose to their ears as they climbed — the only sound in the vast silence of the night.

Their destination was soon plain — a half-ruined stone cottage in a hollow of the cliffs. Was this, then, the spot where Ni had planned that they should die?

A rough road, dropping down towards the little ruin from the heights beyond, led to the broken cottage, and as they approached, Dene saw that a dark saloon car was drawn up near the building. He recognised it as the car in which Ni had come to Moncrieff's house to spy out the land — as he imagined now the reason for Ni's visit to have been.

Weeds choked the tumbled doorway through which he and Julie were thrust, and rank weeds grew up through the gaps in the rotting floorboards. Above, the dim starlight filtered down through the broken slate roof. Ahead, beyond a decaying door that sagged drunkenly on rusted hinges, a light of some kind was burning, candle-light, judging from the wavering glow.

'This the best hospitality you can offer, Ni?' asked Dene.

Stooping, he entered the lighted door-way in answer to a gesture of one of his captor's guns. The low room was better preserved than most of the crumbling building, its ceiling almost intact and the floorboards not yet rotten. A wooden shutter closed the window-opening, and a deal table and a chair with a broken back stood in the centre of the room. A pair of candles stood on the table, in the necks of bottles.

'The drawing-room, eh?' murmured Dene.

And then a quick ejaculation broke from his lips as he caught sight of two figures in the room.

One, the chauffeur whose face he had glimpsed at the wheel of Ni's car earlier that night. The other, Arnold White, lying bound against the wall, staring across at them with intent, startled eyes.

'Mr. Dene!' he heard White breathe. 'What in hell — '

White's eyes swung towards the graceful figure of Mlle. Julie. He recognised her, and his amazement doubled.

How White came to be there, a prisoner like themselves in the hands of Ni, Dene had no means of guessing. It was clear, however, that White had been there some time, with the chauffeur left to guard him. The pale blue eyes met Arnold's with a sardonic smiling light.

'This seems our unlucky night!' he murmured.

Ni was muttering to his men, and two of them vanished back along the passage outside. The Korean turned to Dene, and his eyes were merciless.

'You will remain here!' he said harshly. 'For a while. I need the car for the present. But later you will be taken for a little ride — you and the lady — a ride from which you will not return!'

'Putting us on the spot, eh?' drawled Dene. 'Taking us somewhere where our bodies can be hidden nicely. You think of everything, don't you, Ni?'

Ni stabbed his gun smilingly into Dene's side.

'Go over to that wall!' he commanded.

Dene obeyed — he was too old a hand to argue with a gun when his arms were bound. Ni glanced at Mlle. Julie, and the girl followed. The pair of them stood by White, and the man who was evidently to be their guard until the return of the car — one of the men from the *Sea Witch* — settled himself in the broken chair near the door, and dragged the table in front of him, between his prisoners and their sole way of retreat. With a grin on his swarthy face, he drew out a couple of deep-barrelled automatics and laid them on the table before him.

'They'll be safe with me,' he growled.

The chauffeur had left the room with the others now. Ni paused in the doorway, fat, yellow, evil, staring across the guard's shoulder and the table at which he sat, between the three bound captives and the door. A slow smile crept out upon the Korean's face.

'Au revoir, mademoiselle!' he whispered, with hideous softness. 'So long, Mr. Dene! I have business now to do. Urgent business. But soon I shall return, when you will enjoy, I trust, that little ride of which we spoke.'

The soft tones changed abruptly, altered to a malignant rasp:

'There is an ancient, disused mine some miles from here. The shaft is deep — deep! It will hold your bodies safe, undiscovered, for eternity. Yes, a deep, safe grave for you fools who thought to interfere with my plans! Fools — fools — '

He broke off sharply, bowed stiffly, and turned abruptly on his heel. They heard his quick footsteps hurry over the decaying boards outside. A few moments later the hum of a car's powerful engines came to their ears, roared loudly, and moved away through the night, dying to a distant drone that was lost at last in the great silence.

'Wonder where the hound's gone?' queried Dene aloud. 'Moncrieff's house?'

He glanced down quizzically at White.

'Well,' he asked, 'what's your yarn?'

Arnold still looked white and ill — still amazed, too, by the arrival at the ruined cottage to which he had been brought a prisoner of Dene, also a captive in Ni's hands; equally amazed by the presence of Mlle. Julie.

Julie, for her part, was almost as astonished at the sight of White. His presence made it clear to her that Trevor Lowe was in the affair, a thing she had not previously suspected.

'So!' she murmured softly, her dark, alluring eyes bent down on White's huddled form, with its white up-staring face. 'Monsieur White — of all people! So my good friend, the bon Monsieur Lowe, the English dramatist — he also is at work in these affairs!'

Her eyes turned to Dene. The Secret

Service man nodded.

'Sure, Lowe's in it! Bit of a knock for you, eh, Julie?'

She shrugged.

'M'sieur Lowe, he is very clever man,' she admitted smilingly. 'But what would you? It would seem, too, mes amis, that before long these things will no longer interest us.'

'If Ni succeeds in getting us out to that mine?' muttered Dene. 'By thunder, you're right!'

In laconic tones he gave White a brief explanation of their presence there, and learnt from him how he also came to be a prisoner in the Korean's hands. Their captor, his chair tilted back against the doorpost, a cigarette drooping from his lips, watched them. He was a big man, as most of Ni's satellites seemed to be, with a low-browed, heavy face and a nose that had not only been broken, but badly broken, at some time during his no doubt unsavoury career. His rather bloodshot eyes were fixed appraisingly upon the graceful, slender figure of Mlle. Julie as he sucked his cigarette.

Julie fastened her eyes upon him, and the guard shifted uneasily for a moment in his chair, and glanced away. The girl shot Dene a swift glance, and moved quietly forward toward the table.

Instantly one of the guard's gnarled hands went out to the pair of guns.

'Get back to that wall!' he growled.

'But, m'sieur, surely you do not mind if I sit on the table — near you!' Julie's melodious voice was persuasive. 'You do not mind that? I am oh, so tired! You must, please, let me sit down — no?'

He stared at her suspiciously. Julie laughed, and her laugh was soft and very sweet.

'You are not afraid of me, mon ami? Of me — a woman? Oh, la-la!'

She was still advancing languorously towards the table. Dene and White watched, motionless. They knew of old that Julie had power to enchant the most unlikely victims.

'By thunder,' breathed Dene, 'if she can get him soft — '

The guard was surveying Julie scowlingly.

'Afraid of you?' he echoed. 'Afraid of you be hanged! O.K., you can sit there if you like. But if you're thinking you'll vamp me into letting you go, you can finish your dream right now.'

'Vamp — what is that?' Julie seated herself with easy, lissom grace on the corner of the rough table, despite her bound arms.

Her dark, fascinating eyes were fastened upon the burly ruffian at the other side of the table innocently enough.

'Vamp! I guess there's no need to teach you!' grinned the man evilly. 'But no woman makes a fool of me. Not even a Frenchy! I guess I'm vamp-proof.'

Julie sighed. Her eyes seemed troubled, frightened.

'And I had hoped you would be kind to me,' she said sadly.

'Yeah, I thought that was it!' nodded the guard sourly.

He shifted the guns closer to him, out of Julie's range even if her arms had been free.

'Perhaps you give me a cigarette, m'sieur?'

'Sure, if it'll keep your pretty mouth shut!'

The guard took a cigarette packet from his pocket and leant over to place one between her lips.

'So you think, at least, that I am pretty, m'sieur?'

'You're a good-looker all right,' agreed the guard reluctantly. His eyes were intent upon her, with a new curiosity, as he held out a match to her cigarette. 'And you've got pluck — I'll say that. But women mean nothin' to me!' he added hastily. 'No woman ever made a fool of me yet.'

He leered up at her.

Julie blew a thin stream of smoke from her red lips. Her delicate perfume touched her captor's nostrils — seemed to unsettle him, for he stirred restlessly in his chair.

'Guess I've got to do as the chief says.' There was almost a note of vague apology in the growling voice. 'I'm left to look after you — you and those two!' He nodded across the candlelit room. 'If I was to let you go, lady, I'd be for it! He thinks you're dangerous to this game he's on — '

'I — a woman! M'sieur, I think I am dangerous to no one!' pleaded Julie softly.

Michael Dene could have laughed aloud, had Julie been playing for stakes less grim. For there were not many embassies and consuls in Europe other than those of her own nationality, who had not had cause at one time or another to dread the cool resource and daring of Mlle. Julie of the French Secret Service.

'The chief's orders!' growled the big ruffian.

But the close proximity of her alluring femininity seemed definitely to unsettle him. He was avoiding her eyes now, and Julie edged a little along the table, a trifle closer, bent a slender, silken shoulder towards him.

'But, m'sieur, you are a white man! How can you help a yellow man — in this? You are big, strong. You have no need to be afraid of Monsieur Ni! You are afraid of no one — '

There was a challenge in her words, and it had its effect.

'Who says I'm afraid of Ni?' snarled the guard. 'You're crazy! I'm not afraid of any sneaking lemon-coloured hound on this earth!'

Julie laughed softly.

'You talk bravely now — now that he is not here! And yet, m'sieur, you are afraid to let me go! Afraid of what he would do in punishment! La, you are a coward!'

The big ruffian glared at her.

'Chuck it!' he growled. 'I can see your little game. Trying to fool me into letting you go, aren't you? You and your pals as well — '

'Blague!' Julie interrupted with an impatient exclamation and a contemptuous shrug of her slim shoulders as she glanced with seeming scorn at Dene and White. 'They are nothing to me! Let them stay here! I care nothing! They are not friends of mine, these Englishmen. But if you were kind — if you were to let me go — '

In the wavering candlelight her beauty was breathtaking as she bent down towards him, her slender, bound hands grasping the edge of the table to support herself, her soft melodious voice strangely irresistible. The guard stared into the eyes that held his own, fascinated by Mlle. Julie in that moment as so many other men had been fascinated — to their cost — by the beautiful girl-spy from the Quai D'Orsay.

'Well,' he muttered hoarsely, 'what if I do let you go?'

His big hand pawed her shoulder. For the moment he was lost to all else but the slender loveliness of the French girl, bent languorously towards him. She drew away, and he stepped round the end of the table with a long stride and caught her as she jumped from the table with both hands on her shoulders. Her eyes danced up into his; her lips were parted, breathless.

'I'll do it!' he told her thickly. 'I'll let you go! That yellow hound — '

Something in her eyes checked him. She was looking past him now, and in a flash he sensed the trap into which he had fallen. With an oath he swung round, to leap for his guns, but already Michael Dene was by the table, one of the heavy weapons held in his bound hands, twisted behind his back to cover the dumbfounded guard.

'Put 'em up!' jerked out Dene. 'That's

the style! And don't get the idea I can't aim straight because my hands aren't free! I'll increase your weight with lead if you shift an inch!'

With his huge arms raised on high the burly ruffian switched his gaze slowly from Dene to Mlle. Julie, and as his eyes rested on the girl their bloodshot glare was inhuman in its fury. Julie laughed very softly.

'So no woman has ever made a fool of you, m'sieur!' she cried banteringly. 'But you were easy!'

Moving quickly round the table, she twisted her arms round to take the second gun. Except for a single spitting oath, the guard seemed incapable of speech.

'Get over and untie him!' rasped Dene, with a nod towards Arnold. 'And move fast!'

For a moment or two only did the man hesitate. Then he turned without a word, livid-faced, and crossed to the corner where White was still sitting propped against the wall.

Like a man in a daze, the big scoundrel bent down and with a clasp-knife slashed through the cords that bound White's ankles and wrists.

Arnold staggered to his feet.

'Thanks!' he said dryly. 'That's a lot better!'

With two guns covering him the man knew that he was beaten, even though the guns were held in the hands of a man and a girl whose arms were bound behind their backs. He seemed to recognise that both Dene and the girl-spy were more than sufficiently expert with a weapon of that nature to have floored him, nevertheless.

He made no audible protest as White snatched the clasp-knife from his hand and crossed towards Mlle. Julie and the Secret Service man. But his eyes were inhuman as he watched their bonds slashed through, and at last he broke into a torrent of vivid oaths, his whole face contorted with helpless animal-rage.

'You can cut that out, Angel-Face!' rasped Dene savagely.

The stream of oaths went on unchecked. With a long stride Dene placed himself within range, and his left fist slammed home on the man's heavy jaw. He went down with a crash, lay glaring up at Dene with a bloodshot glitter in his eyes, his big figure spreadeagled at the spy's feet.

'Get up!' grated the Secret Service man. 'And keep your mouth shut this time!'

The man rose with sullen fury, and Arnold lashed his wrists. Slipping the gun into his pocket Dene stepped forward and ran his hands through the pockets of Julie's victim. He was not looking for weapons; it had occurred to him that there might be some clue on this satellite of Ni's to the mystery of the ship on which had been hidden — as he knew now, having forced the information from Ni himself — the stolen Anglo-Japanese treaty that he was out to recover, at any cost, for the British Government, the missing treaty that meant so much not only to England but to Europe, and which the French Government were also fighting to obtain, through the agency of their cleverest and most charming spy.

A bulky pocket-case of worn, tattered leather rewarded his efforts. He pulled it unceremoniously from the man's inner pocket, ran hastily through its contents. There were various papers of no importance to Dene, and then, almost the last that he examined, brought a quick gleam to his eyes, a gleam of eager satisfaction.

His hunch had been on the mark!

A folded sheet of paper, torn from a ship's log-book. Scrawled across it were a number of Oriental characters that he recognised as being Japanese, and his knowledge of Japanese caligraphy was not sufficient to translate them, but beneath these were seven letters that meant much, written by a hand that seemed unused to the tracing of Roman lettering, the letters joined together into one word:

'OKIMARU'

'Ciel!' he heard Julie breathe. 'A discovery, mon ami!'

'Looks like a discovery all right — maybe a useful discovery, when this has been translated!' agreed Dene, thrusting the paper into his pocket. 'I can see I shall have to rub up my Japanese — '

His words snapped off.

The hum of a distant car had come abruptly to their ears.

'Ni's back!' breathed White.

'Ni and the rest of 'em!' muttered Dene, and glanced doubtfully at Julie.

But for the girl, he and White might have made some attempt to trap Ni, big though the odds against them were, if, as they expected, Ni had with him his bunch of ruffians from the *Sea Witch*. But to risk letting Julie fall again into the hands of the Korean he did not mean to do. That consideration — and that alone — could stand between Dene and the immediate job on hand.

Strange though the relationship between the British Secret Service man and the girl from the Quai D'Orsay was, though they were deadly rivals in this affair, as they had been in so many others, their personal feelings were those of two rival competitors in the most fascinating game on earth — the great game of international Intelligence. Reckless, daring, utterly unknown to fear though Julie was, Dene's every natural instinct was to see her safe from the clutches of the mysterious Mr. Tsu Ni — even though that meant ensuring her freedom to war against himself in their struggle for the missing treaty.

He gripped her arm.

'Come on, Julie! We won't try to handle Ni's crowd — too many of 'em this time!'

He thrust her towards the door.

The hum of the rapidly approaching car was loud now. As the three of them hurried along the dim passage outside, towards the tumbledown entrance of the ruined cottage, the faint starlight streaming in through the gaps in the roof above — leaving their late guard cursing volubly once more — they could hear the car swinging down into the little hollow in which the building stood.

They ran out through the weed-choked doorway.

With the car approaching from the rear of the ruin, they were still safe from observation. Dene's hand had dropped to the pocket where his new weapon lay, as he led the way swiftly round the corner of the dilapidated little building into the dark shadows on the right. They halted there, drawn back against the broken wall, and heard the car draw to a halt by the entrance they had just left. Evidently it had been travelling without lights, for there was no glare of headlamps.

They heard men descending, muttered voices, the slamming of the car doors; heard footsteps echo dully on the rotten boards within the cottage. In a few seconds now the discovery of their escape would be made.

Dene peered round the angle of the wall, and now his gun was in his hand again.

He made out the figure of the chauffeur standing by the car, lighting a cigarette, his lean, lantern-jawed face revealed clearly by the tiny flare of the match. Another man was disappearing into the broken doorway.

'Come on!' hissed Dene, and leapt round the corner of the building, Arnold White at his heels.

The chauffeur was leisurely shaking the still lighted match to extinguish it, puffing at the cigarette between his lips. He froze for a moment at sight of the two dim figures racing towards him — leapt back instinctively, his mouth opened to cry out in startled bewilderment, his right hand shooting to his hip. But before he could whip out the gun, or shout, he was reeling back stupidly, with an ugly mark showing where Dene's automatic had crashed down, butt-ended, between his eyes.

The chauffeur thudded against the wall, and gave way at the knees, going down with a groan. At the same instant, from within the building, an excited shout came to their ears.

But already White was scrambling into the driving-seat.

The engine roared out as Dene dragged open the car door, and the lithe figure of Mlle. Julie leapt in. He followed her, and the door slammed as the car backed in a jolting curve, to turn for the road.

Swift figures sprang into view in the shadows of the cottage doorway as White slammed the gear through and the car curved away towards the rough road. A tongue of flame gashed the darkness, and there was a thud as the bullet struck the body of the car.

'Step on it!' drawled Dene.

White was 'stepping on it' with a vengeance. The powerful car hurtled over the rough surface at breakneck speed, climbing out of the hollow with a farewell fusillade whining after it.

There was a low laugh from Mlle Julie. 'Voilà!' she murmured gaily. 'So we do not finish in that deep mine of which the M'sieur Ni so kindly spoke!'

'Not this journey,' nodded Dene comfortably, and laughed deeply. He glanced at the slim figure at his side. 'Tell me this — how did you come to be on board that yacht tonight?'

'I was watching the house,' she confessed with an enigmatical smile. 'I had left my car, with my chauffeur, some little distance away, mon ami — so I was all alone. Two of Ni's men were watching too. They surprised me, and I had no chance to use my automatique — my gun. I was taken out to the yacht — '

She broke off with a smiling shrug.

'You know the rest, M'sieur! And but for you — '

'Well, we're fifty-fifty!' grinned Dene. 'But for you vamping Angel-Face so cleverly, there'd be a thundering different yarn to tell!' He surveyed her curiously as she met his eyes in the dim interior of the speeding car. 'Why were you watching Moncrieff's house, Julie? Why have you bought it, eh? What's that house got to do with the *Oki Maru?*'

'Those are very blunt questions, M'sieur Dene!' she answered merrily. 'Pardon me if I do not answer them, mon cher ami.'

'No, I didn't somehow think you would!' grunted Dene, and grinned crookedly.

The car had reached a better-surfaced road, half a mile or so farther on, when White at last halted the big car.

They were well clear of pursuit now.

White glanced over his shoulder at Dene and Julie with a questioning look.

'Any idea where we are?' he asked.

'None in the world,' answered the Secret Service man, peering out of the window at the dark, lonely countryside with the great mountains rising in the distance to the stars. 'But we can't be far from Moncrieff's place. I — '

The words choked in his throat.

Something had come pressing gently into his side. He stared down, and saw that it was Julie's gun, the weapon she had brought with her from the ruined cottage, held steadily to his jacket by her slim white hand.

'Forgive me, vieux ami!' Her soft voice was amused, but quite definitely determined. There was in her dark eyes a look that Dene knew of old — a look that meant Julie was not to be trifled with at that moment. 'Before we part, m'sieur,' she continued smilingly, 'I must request you to hand over to me that interesting paper you have in your pocket! The paper with the Japanese writing, m'sieur, that you took from the man I had to — what you call it? — 'vamp' a short while ago! I think it tells something of the *Oki Maru*; and I must have it, m'sieur, at once!'

12

Battling Wits!

Michael Dene stared down at the gleaming weapon thrust so uncompromisingly into his side rather blankly. Then an explosive exclamation broke from him.

'By the great Caesar!' he ejaculated.

She laughed softly. White, staring back through the open glass partition that separated the driving seat from the rear of the car, could not see Julie's weapon, but he realised what had happened, and he, too, gave a startled ejaculation. But unarmed as he was, he was powerless to intervene. For already Julie's pretty manicured hand had coolly taken Dene's gun from his pocket, and held that on her knees with her left hand, while her right kept the second weapon thrust warningly into the big Englishman's side.

'S'il vous plaît, m'sieur!' she commanded calmly, her smiling eyes fastened upon Dene's startled face. 'I mean it, my friend. Remember, our truce we agreed should last until we reached shore from the yacht! It is over now. I have my country's work to think of — and I must have that paper.'

The note of quiet determination in her voice was not to be denied. She had taken him off his guard, and he was helplessly in her power, with that rim of steel nosing against his jacket while her dainty finger rested on the trigger.

And what she said was true enough. Their truce was to have lasted until they reached shore, but after that —

'I have to take off my hat to you, Julie!' growled Dene, and there was a certain grim amusement in his voice, despite their chagrin. 'I believe you would plug me, too, for your country's sake, if I tried to — '

He broke off. Like lightning his left hand had dropped to the gun at his side, thrusting it aside and up, his fingers knotted like steel around the slender wrist. But instantly her left hand whipped round with the second gun, covering him.

For some moments they were quite still, Dene's hand locked on her wrist. But that second gun was an unanswerable argument, and slowly he released his grasp of her right hand.

'You win, Julie!'

'Mais oui! I think I do!' she smiled mockingly. But she did not attempt to take the paper he had drawn from his pocket and held out to her — that would have meant losing control of one of her guns. 'Non, non, m'sieur! I am not so foolish as that! Throw it from the car!'

Dene stared at her nonplussed. He had intended to make a grab for her remaining gun when she laid down the other in order to snatch the precious paper. But he was not to be given a chance of that!

Whether or not Julie would actually have shot him had he refused, he could not feel sure. He believed she would, though certainly not to kill. But he could read in her eyes that her determination to obtain possession of the cryptic paper was such that she would, if necessary, have put a bullet in his arm, to cripple his resistance. He could hardly blame her. He had a man's strength, she a woman's physical weakness. In circumstances such as these, she had to even up the handicap by any means available.

Bitter though it was to have to obey, there was no use in courting a wounded arm or shoulder that might put him out of action for a long while, and cost him far more than the loss of the paper she demanded. For a moment his eyes met White's, as a fresh idea came to him. And Arnold read their message.

'You clever little cheat!' he murmured appraisingly. 'O.K., Julie — '

He turned to the window, as if to lower it in order to fling out the paper in obedience to her orders. But as he turned, the car's purring engines thundered loud — it leapt forward as White slammed in the clutch, gathered speed with lightning acceleration along the dark road; and Dene smilingly returned the paper to his pocket.

'What now, Julie?' he drawled. 'You've got the guns, my dear, and you know how to use 'em only too thundering well for my liking! But we're doing about sixty miles an hour at the moment! Even if you shot me dead to get that paper, m' dear, you couldn't jump out without breaking your pretty neck! And if you were crazy enough to slug White, we'd all crash to blazes together!'

He gave a deep chuckle. For the moment even Julie appeared at a loss, as she stared at him with angrily flashing eyes. He had beaten her in this battle of wits — beaten her on her own ground!

'Shoot away!' grinned Michael Dene.

Where the road led, they did not know. But that it went roughly in the direction of the house they wanted, seemed sure enough. Moncrieff's place — Llanyllyn, as the name of the house was — was their desired destination for more reasons than one! Not only did Dene wish to circumscribe Julie's future actions in the matter of the lost treaty by holding her a semi-prisoner at the house; he was grimly eager to get to the business end of a telephone, to instruct the police at Caermawr to patrol the roads in search of Ni and his men — to get the Korean and his white and yellow satellites netted in a human trap, as well as to return himself, if possible with Lowe and the constables at the house, to the cottage on the cliffs, on Ni's trail.

He looked into the dark, lovely eyes so near his own with a sardonic smile.

'What now, Julie?' he drawled again.

Her face was set.

'You are clever, m'sieur!' But the guns in her hands did not lower. 'But all the same, you will give me that paper — now! Maintenant!'

'If you think it'll be any use to you, you're welcome!' chuckled Dene.

He took out the folded log-sheet, and tossed it into her lap.

'Put your hands above your head!' she ordered.

Dene obeyed, tense and watchful. If Julie gave him the slightest chance, he would have both her wrists in a vice-like grip — and she knew it. Without putting down the gun in that hand, with her left hand she succeeded in thrusting the paper into a pocket of her dress, while her right hand covered him with her other weapon, its barrel levelled significantly at his shoulder.

The car was travelling faster now — nearer seventy than sixty, along the straight cliff road; White was taking no chances of Julie's daring a leap from the speeding vehicle, and was holding the accelerator down in a way that made such a leap out of the question even for the daring French girl. To their right, the rugged coast-line was curving in nearer to the road in a wide bay. And suddenly Julie saw her chance.

So swiftly that Arnold had no time to tighten his grip upon the wheel of the car, she had half-risen, leaning through the open window behind his head, her flashing hands darting to the big steering-wheel. Her thumbs still thrust through the trigger-guards of the weapons they held, her slim fingers gripped the wheel and wrenched it round despite his hastily tightened grasp upon it. The big car swung off the road on to the level turf between it and the cliff-edge — roared at racing speed towards the jagged brink.

Even Dene was so dumbfounded by

her action that for the instant he sat motionless. Then, as his arms shot out to drag her back, it was too late; already they were tearing for the cliff-edge, with Julie sinking back in her seat, whipping round her twin guns to cover him once more.

For a split-second it flashed into his mind that Julie, for some inexplicable reason, deliberately wished to send the car, with all three of them, over the edge to a certain death. Then, as White madly jammed on the brakes, he understood!

He had no choice but to brake for dear life — no room to turn the car on that narrow tongue of cliff, at that breakneck speed. And Julie had risked the chance of sheer disaster, to force him into stopping the car at any cost.

Bumping and swaying, the heavy saloon drew to an abrupt standstill, within twenty yards of the cliff edge. Julie already had the door open, and before the car had stopped she had leapt out. Now her voice rang out in crisp command:

'Alight, mes amis!'

Backed as her order was by those guns in her hands, Dene and White had no choice but to obey the incisive order. They stepped out on to the grass, the French girl surveying them with a cool, mocking little smile. Across the cliffs, the sea-wind came blowing freshly, stirring the beautiful bronze hair of the girl spy in dancing waves.

'Hell!' jerked out Dene.

'March!' commanded Julie. And the two unarmed men moved reluctantly away from the car, at the same time that the French girl drew towards it.

She climbed quickly into the driving seat, sat covering them now with a single gun, the other laid on the seat beside her. By the cliff-edge, Dene and White turned and faced her. The mocking smile still curled her delicately rouged lips as she surveyed them.

'Au revoir, m'sieurs!'

Arnold had stopped the engine. Julie pressed the self-starter, and once more it roared to life. She slipped the gear-lever into reverse; and driving with one hand, backed rapidly towards the road.

'And she's got that paper!' grated the Secret Service man. 'Hell! There's no licking Julie, bless her — the pretty little knave!'

There was a rueful chagrin in his eyes as he and White watched the car turn near the road, lurch on to the roadway and speed away into the darkness. The sound of its exhaust was lost on the wind.

Arnold grinned crookedly.

'She's made us look silly this time, all right,' he confessed wryly.

Michael Dene burst into a sudden laugh of genuine amusement. Then his mouth shut like a trap in a grim, hard line.

'But we'll beat her yet!' he muttered. 'We've got to — at any cost!'

13

The Crouching Man

Trevor Lowe, his face thoughtful, sat by the window of an upper room in the house where Sir Matthew Moncrieff had met his mysterious end the previous night, and stared with absent eyes across the grounds towards the distant line of cliffs. His pipe was between his teeth, and a slow coil of smoke rose ceilingwards from the well-filled bowl.

It was mid-day.

Though in falling from the roof he had crashed his head against the trunk of the tree that had saved his life, and had been stunned and senseless when he had been brought to earth by the police constables, he had not taken long to recover from his experience. But Inspector Richards, whom the hunted man had knifed on the roofs, had had to be taken by ambulance to the hospital at Caermawr, soon after dawn. The inspector was in a bad condition — lucky to have escaped with his life.

Before dawn, Dene and White had arrived back at the house with their startling story. But Ni and the men from the *Sea Witch* seemed to have slipped through the police cordon that had hastily been thrown round the district in response to a telephone message to the station at Caermawr; for the birds had flown when Dene, White and Lowe, together with half a dozen constables and an inspector, recently arrived to take over from Richards, had reached the tumble-down cottage where Ni and his satellites had last been seen. Yet their launch had still been on the beach blow.

Nothing, either, had been seen of Mlle. Julie. The French girl had vanished as utterly as Ni for the time being — though they could feel sure that it would not be long before Julie's secret operations became once more apparent.

Lowe glanced round as the door opened. The big figure of Dene stood framed in the doorway.

Dene had been out with Inspector Williams and a constable to inspect the stranded *Sea Witch* before the rising tide lifted her from the rocks and sunk her, using for the purpose Ni's own launch. He had not entertained much hope that they would find on board the yacht anything of use to them, and the expression on his face as he entered the room where Lowe had been so deep in thought seemed to bear out his expectations.

'No luck?' queried Lowe.

'None!' growled the other. 'Didn't even get aboard her. While we were on the way out to her, she took the plunge! Went down stern first, as quiet as a seal. No report come in of Ni having been seen by the police patrols?'

'None.'

Dene had crossed to the window, stood staring out towards the cliffs with a knotted frown, his jaw tight set.

'Looks as if we've hit a blank wall, Lowe — for the moment. If only Julie hadn't been so darned smart and got away with that Jap scrawl — '

'That was certainly unfortunate,' agreed

Lowe, with a dry glance at the Secret Service man; and for a moment a smile touched his lips.

'We know nothing!' growled Dene savagely. 'Nothing, except that the stolen draft-treaty was on board the *Oki Maru* when she did the vanishing trick, and that the *Oki Maru* didn't founder in that storm after all! Can't have done, since that chronometer turned up safe and sound in Birkenhead! And we know that both Julie and Ni have some reason to believe that this very house is an important factor in the mystery! Though who Ni is — '

'I can tell you that,' broke in Lowe quietly, and Dene swung round to stare at him. 'I've just had a telephone report through from London. I got in touch with Shadgold last night, telling him to make inquiries. Here's his report. I jotted it down.'

He picked up a notebook that was lying open on the table by his chair, and handed it to Dene.

' 'Tsu Ni,'' read Dene aloud. ' 'Korean. Address, 101, Berkeley Square. Educated in England, Oxford University. Lived in

England many years, occasionally visiting Korea and Tokio. Well known in wealthy Eastern colony in London. Owns large properties in Korea, also large interest in Hoang Hi Trading Co., Ltd., of 74, Pentan Street, London Wall. Bank, Eastern and British Commercial Bank.''

'H'm!' He handed the notebook back to Lowe. 'So that visiting-card of his wasn't fake! But I don't see that this information's a fat lot of use to us, candidly. We don't know why — '

'I think I do know why,' interrupted Lowe softly. 'In fact, I am beginning to see daylight! Not very clearly as yet, perhaps, but the first gleams!'

He puffed a heavy coiling smoke-ring to the ceiling, watched it break against the plaster.

'I have also been talking to Shadgold, at the Yard, by 'phone,' he went on 'You remember that dead Oriental found murdered by the railway line between London and Liverpool? Believed at the Yard to have been murdered by the second mate of the *Oki Maru*, then chucked from the train.'

'I remember,' nodded Dene. 'Never identified the murdered man, did they?'

'No, Shadgold is still trying to find out who the dead man was. I think I could tell him!'

'The deuce you could!' ejaculated Dene. 'Who?'

'The second mate of the *Oki Maru* himself!' chuckled Lowe.

'But the second mate joined the ship and sailed in her!'

'He was supposed to have done. But I've been considering that case, since it seems possible it may have some bearing on these other matters. And the solution to that struck me almost at once, when I went over the details. Consider, Dene — two men, Koreans, travelling on that train; one murders the other; surely it would be too big a coincidence to imagine for a moment that they met by chance, in England, on a long train journey? Obviously the murderer followed his victim, took the train because his victim did, trailing him, waiting his chance — '

'That seems reasonable,' nodded Dene. 'But — '

'And yet we know that the second mate of the *Oki Maru* was travelling on that train to join his ship. Therefore he was not the tracker, but the tracked. He was followed by the would-be murderer. He was attacked. If the mate of the *Oki Maru* had killed his attacker in self-defence during the struggle he has nothing to hide; he would have killed the man in defence of his own life, which lets him out; whereas, if he hushes it up, he puts himself in a terrible position, as any man intelligent enough to have become a second mate would know. I think we can consider it far more probable that the attacker succeeded in his purpose, killed the mate, and then joined the *Oki Maru* in the dead man's identity. He was joining a new ship, we know. He had only to steal the dead man's papers and luggage, and he had no difficulty, since no one on board the *Oki Maru* knows him; and since the ship is sailing more or less immediately, she is almost certain to sail before there is a chance of any agent from the London office, for example, who would recognise the deception, arriving in

Liverpool to do so.'

'Seems reasonable,' agreed Dene again.

'When you come to think of it that way! You mean — '

'It is another fact for us to fit into the bigger scheme,' murmured Lowe. 'From the various facts in our possession we may now make several obvious deductions. Of the two parties at work — apart from ourselves — we can fairly safely assume that, owing to his nationality — the fellow who murdered the second officer of the *Oki Maru* and took the dead man's place, was working for Ni, not for Julie and the French Secret Service.

'It is obvious, as a result, that since Ni's agent was evidently going to such lengths to get on board the *Oki Maru*, that this ship in particular held a significance for him. Therefore, he had not himself got the stolen draft-treaty with him and merely seeking to get out of the country with it. His purpose must have been that he knew the treaty to be on board the *Oki Maru*, and was determined — on Ni's behalf — to get on board in order to obtain it.

'Therefore it was the other party to the affair — our charming young friend Mlle. Julie — who had original possession of the treaty, not Ni. Julie, therefore, was the individual — unless an agent acted for her — who stole the treaty from the Foreign Office. That would certainly be a task after her own heart, eh, Dene?'

'Jove, yes!' muttered the Secret Service man.

'Julie, then, stole the draft of that Anglo-Japanese treaty, and, for some reason of which we are at present ignorant, entrusted it to someone on board the *Oki Maru* for dispatch to its destination. Odd, since the ship was bound for the Yellow Sea; but I think there can be no doubt about it, all the same. Ni, somehow, discovered this fact, and he himself wanted to get possession of it. I think we can deduce what his reason was.'

Lowe picked up the notebook from the table, glancing at the scribbled notes concerning Mr. Tsu Ni of Berkeley Square.

'Large interest in Hoang Hi Trading Co., Ltd.,' he murmured grimly. ''Hoang

Hi,' by the way, is the Chinese name for the Yellow Sea, as you probably know.' Dene nodded. 'Ni owns large properties in Korea in addition. His wealth, in fact, is bound up inescapably with Anglo-Korean trade. Korea, of course, being now a possession of Japan, Korea is vitally affected by the proposed treaty in connection with Anglo-Japanese trading interests. Ni therefore got hold of this killer — probably someone he met in Tokio, for apparently he ran a secret society there at one time.'

'Yes' — Michael Dene crashed a fist down upon the table — 'I'm beginning to grasp things. Julie is, of course, working for France, which is naturally intensely keen to know the substance of that treaty of ours with the Japanese, while Ni is working for the Hoang Hi syndicate — '

'Exactly! If the Hoang Hi crowd could get wise to the substance of that treaty it would enable them, with their vast trading interests worth millions, to anticipate any reciprocal tariff or reduction of tariffs, trading arrangements, and so on, to an extent that might mean millions of yen to them in the money market. An unscrupulous crowd, sticking at nothing in their attempt to get their hands on that treaty in advance of everyone else! Eastern millionaires out to pile wealth on wealth, with that evil scoundrel Ni working their schemes — '

'But why this house?' broke in Dene wonderingly. 'Where does this house come into it at all? That's what beats me.'

Lowe did not for a moment answer. He sat thoughtfully silent. Then he rose and crossed the room to a bookcase by the farther wall. Opening the glass doors, he drew out a bulky volume and laid it on the table — an atlas, as Dene now saw. Lowe turned the pages and flattened the atlas out at a map of Wales.

'The *Oki Maru* vanished, after that single broken SOS message, on her first night out from Liverpool. We don't know what speed she made against the storm, but a reasonable estimate is that she covered about this much of her route before she — vanished! Whatever it was that happened to her — and we know she did not founder in the ordinary way — it occurred — whatever 'it' was — just about here.'

He marked a tiny cross on the coloured sheet with a pencil-point.

'Say she was here when she sent out that SOS that was never finished.' He marked a line at right-angles to the shipping route, to the nearest land. 'And here we are at this very spot — this lonely stretch of coast without a town for miles — the nearest town, in fact, Caermawr. Out there' — he flung a pointing hand out towards the distant horizon, where the sea mingled with the grey sky — 'out there, Dene! Not so many miles off shore, probably! Immediately opposite this house, more or less — that's where the *Oki Maru* was when, on that night of storm, she sent out that last message to the world. That night she was supposed to have foundered — until proof came that she can't be at the bottom of the sea, after all! Significant, to realise that that stretch of sea before us is in all likelihood the same path of ocean as that in which the *Oki Maru* fought the storm! Significant, when we consider that both Ni and Mlle.

232

Julie herself, for some reason that they alone know, persistently connect this house with the lost ship: and when we remember, too, that Shasataka's watch — Shasataka, the captain of the *Oki Maru* — was found by White near the house. What it all means I can't tell you. But we're up against something weird — '

'Think Julie knows what happened to that Jap steamer?' cut in Dene quickly.

Lowe shook his head.

'My idea is that she doesn't — but that Ni does! I'll tell you why. Unless Ni knows more than she does, why should she have wanted to get that paper she collared last night? Not simply to prevent you from knowing something she already knew, or all she would have had to do when it was in her hands was to have destroyed it, as she could easily have done. No, she wanted it herself. She believes Ni has knowledge that would be thundering useful to her — hoped, as you hoped, that that Japanese scrawl might tell it! Well, what can Ni know that Julie doesn't know? Nothing other than the secret to the riddle of the *Oki Maru*!'

'That's so,' agreed Dene.

'What puzzles me,' went on Lowe, dropping into his chair again, 'is why Ni, if he knows where the *Oki Maru* is, doesn't go to her and get what he wants off her. Evidently there is some big obstacle in his way to prevent his doing so. And — why did he come to this house?'

'Lord knows!' growled Dene perplexedly. 'You've cleared the air a good deal, but when it comes to the mystery of the *Oki Maru*, that, by right, should be at the bottom of the sea, yet must still be drifting round somewhere on top of it after all — without a chronometer — well, it beats me to the wide!'

He paced the floor restlessly.

'What about Moncrieff's murder?' he asked suddenly.

'One of Ni's men, who had penetrated this house for that mysterious reason we still don't understand, was sneaking round; Moncrieff saw him, and the fellow murdered Moncrieff to keep him silent. But why the murderer — the fellow we routed later out of the chimney, and who had tried to scare us, as we know now, by scrawling those Japanese characters on the picture in the long gallery — why he was here at all in the first place, is a big problem; the same problem as to why Julie bought this place.'

'Well, I can't imagine even Julie will have the nerve to arrive here to claim her property now!' grinned Dene crookedly. 'That reminds me. Did Miss Delmar get off all right?'

Lowe nodded. Letitia Delmar had left the house that morning with her old housekeeper for Shrewsbury, to stay with friends, to whom Lowe had wired. After her terrible experiences, it had been considered best for her to leave the house where her murdered uncle lay dead, victim of the strange maelstrom of plot and counter-plot that had descended so tragically upon the once peaceful old pile that he had sold for his niece's sake on the eve of his death.

'What are we to do now?' jerked out Dene. 'Ni's vanished — Julie's vanished!'

'We simply wait,' murmured Lowe slowly as his eyes followed his tobacco-smoke to the ceiling. 'Irksome to a man of action, perhaps, but our best game to play. The key to the mystery of the *Oki Maru* lies somewhere in this house. However much Ni knows, however much Julie knows, we hold the ace of trumps at the moment, for we are in this house, to which they are bound, in the end, to come. Of one thing I am sure — we shan't have to wait long before they are drawn here inevitably. Ni will come to this house, Julie will come to this house, like iron filings to a magnet.'

A silence that struck Dene as being oddly electric, tense in its suggestion of invisible forces at work close at hand, followed his quietly spoken words. Dene halted, listening to the chill wind that muttered beneath the eaves. Suddenly his eyes gleamed.

'I believe you're right!' he whispered. 'They'll come!'

★   ★   ★

Inspector Williams, who had replaced the ill-fated Richards as the police officer in charge of the affair of the murder of Sir

Matthew Moncrieff, was a cadaverous individual, tall and bony, with thinning hair and a habit of pulling thoughtfully at his lower lip with a gaunt finger and thumb, who looked considerably more like an old-fashioned lawyers' clerk than a detective-inspector. But, despite his mournful demeanour, he had done his work quietly and efficiently, with much pulling at his elongated lower lip, before returning, soon after midday, to Caermawr, leaving a burly police-sergeant named Owen as police representative at the house.

There was no doubt that the murderer of Sir Matthew Moncrieff had made his escape to the now sunken *Sea Witch*, after his flight from the roofs. And since those from the yacht had disappeared utterly for the time being, until the police patrols now scouring the neighbourhood for them reported some clue to their whereabouts or some such information came in from another station, there was nothing for the mournful inspector to do.

Sergeant Owen was a very different person from his superior. Big and florid, with a massive waistline and cheerful countenance, he exuded honest good nature. Trevor Lowe and Dene, coming across the sergeant, sunning himself in the grounds soon after the inspector's departure, were greeted with a beaming, respectful grin.

'Very nasty affair this, sirs!' he announced cheerfully. 'Knew Sir Matthew well. Nicer gentleman you couldn't wish to meet.'

'A nasty affair all right, sergeant,' agreed Lowe quietly.

'You know, sir, I've got a theory,' went on the big sergeant in the same cheerful tones. 'There was a big landslide up the coast some time last night, so I've heard. At Moldiff Cove, six miles from here. Always having 'em along this coast. What if these men they want were over at Moldiff Cove, and got caught on the piece of cliff that slid into the sea? They wouldn't have a chance!'

'Sounds almost too good to be likely,' suggested Dene dryly.

'Well, I don't know, sir,' beamed Sergeant Owen. 'Just an idea of mine, sir. A big landslide takes in a wide stretch of cliff, you know. There was a landslide here a few weeks back that they said carried — well, I forget the figures, but it was thousands of tons of cliff that collapsed like a kid's sand castle. Over there, it was.' He gestured vaguely towards the cliffs. 'Still, it was only an idea, sir. Don't suppose there's anything in it, as you say.'

The big sergeant dismissed his theory as cheerfully as he had first presented it.

'Looks like being a useful fellow in a rough house, that sergeant,' murmured Dene as he and Lowe went on. They were on their way to make another search of the line of shrubs in which White, the previous night, had found the bewildering clue of the watch of the captain of the *Oki Maru*. Arnold himself had driven over to Caermawr to fill up the Rolls' petrol-tank and bring back a supply of extra tins. 'Yes, he'd be useful in a rough house, with shoulders that size. And, by Jove, we may need him badly!' he finished grimly.

'Very possibly!' agreed Lowe.

Convinced though they were that Ni would come to the house sooner or later — and more likely sooner, when he might imagine his return would be least expected — they had deliberately not mentioned their expectations to the inspector, nor asked for a posse of police to be left. If Ni came, they wanted to handle him their own way, unhampered by police red-tape.

Their search of the bushes that had provided the clue of the watch was fruitless, minutely though they examined every inch of ground. It was nearly half an hour later that they gave up the task, convinced that they had missed nothing.

Heavy clouds were rolling up over the sea, blotting out the sinking sun, as they strode back along the flagged path towards the french windows, by which they had entered the garden. As they reached the windows, Lowe halted abruptly, staring across the darkening lawn.

'What the deuce — '

The Secret Service man at his side stared in the direction of Lowe's suddenly intent gaze.

Vague and dim though it was, in the shadow of the clump of trees by the corner of the big lawn something that was visible there had come into their view, something that looked queerly like a crouching human figure, peering back at them across the wide stretch of lawn.

'Someone there!' said Lowe quickly.

The next moment he and the Secret Service man were crossing the lawn at a run on silent feet.

The figure did not shift — seemed not to have noticed their approach. And then, as they drew nearer, they saw — knew what that crouching figure was.

Slumped on his knees, shoulder supported against one of the dark fir-boles, the helmeted head fallen back askew, mouth agape, and eyes half-open as if staring dully up at them, was a uniformed figure — the dead body of Police-sergeant Owen!

14

Nightfall

Used though they both were to the spectacle of violent death, the horror of their discovery turned them cold for the instant. Only a few minutes ago the genial sergeant had been chatting to them by the french windows. Now just a thing of lifeless clay . . .

With the chill wind from the sea whispering in the darkening firs, they stood staring down at the dead thing at their feet with a sense for the moment of fantastic unreality.

'My God — '

No need to convince themselves that the uniformed figure was indeed dead. Both had recognised the certain death in those half-open eyes. But Lowe dropped swiftly beside the huddled form and felt the heart. The dead man was warm, but there was no stirring of life within the big frame.

'Knifed!' he muttered, pointing to an

ugly stain in the back of the uniform.

A sound from the direction of the house caused them to swing round. It was White, back from Caermawr. He came striding across to them, and horror leapt into his face.

'Get that fellow Rice, the chauffeur, to help you carry the poor fellow into the house!' rasped Lowe. 'And telephone Caermawr police-station.'

Already he and Dene were searching for the murderer's trail, Lowe with a small pocket flash-lamp piercing the darkening shadows under the trees.

Arnold hurried away to fetch Rice.

Rain had fallen at dawn, and the lawn was soft in places. It was Dene who first happened on one of the murderer's footprints, faintly traced on the damp grass — a footprint too small to have been that of the dead police-sergeant.

They found another — and another. The faint footprints led towards a large group of trees at the back of the spacious lawn, and there they found one perfectly clear footprint in a patch of mud.

What had brought the unseen killer to

the house again was the problem that held, they knew, the key to the whole grim riddle surrounding the house. The man must have come for some mysterious secret purpose as before, and the sergeant had seen him, and been knifed — as Sir Matthew Moncrieff had been knifed — to silence him.

'One of Ni's men for sure — or even Ni himself!' muttered Dene. 'You said he'd come again, and by heaven he has!'

That last footprint, in the patch of mud by the larger circle of trees, was the last of the trail.

After that, nothing. The trail ended there, and, despite their minute search of all the ground, they could find no further footprints or sign to show the direction of his going. It was dry under the trees, and the ground took no impression.

They returned to the spot where the body had been found.

Both were silent, and in their eyes a gleam almost of savagery as they scoured the scene of the foul crime that had been the latest act of the unknown visitor to the house. There had been something infinitely pathetic in the sight of the dead sergeant, and both men were possessed of a mood of cold ferocity, of relentless determination to get the killer.

The secretary joined them. The dead man had been borne into the house, and Rice, the chauffeur, and old Hart, the butler, had been two unnerved men. The old butler's voice had held a note of hysterical horror as he had cried huskily, with shaking fists:

'It's fiends' work — fiends' work! There are fiends that come and go at will in this house!'

White had calmed him to some extent, but he saw that the old man could not be allowed to stay another night under that sinister roof, for his own sake.

'Found anything?' muttered Arnold.

'That's the way he went — over towards those other trees!' said Lowe. 'There the trail is lost. I'm hoping we may find some clue yet, though — Ah!'

He broke off with a soft ejaculation. His eyes were fastened on the ground near the spot where the dead sergeant had been found.

White looked down quickly, but he could see nothing to have brought the queer look that had leapt into his employer's eyes.

'What is it?'

Lowe did not answer. Stooping, he touched the ground with a lean fore-finger, and as he rose again there was, as Arnold saw, a smear of grey mud.

'Oletonian subsoil!' Arnold heard him murmur in surprise.

There was a tone of tense interest in the dramatist's words. Taking a sheet of paper from his pocket, he smeared the mud on to it and examined it afresh.

'Yes, oletonian undoubtedly. Jove, this is interesting!'

To the secretary's astonishment, he swung abruptly on his heel and hurried across the lawn towards the house, vanishing indoors, with some evident significant purpose.

Dene had been searching the far side of the little clump of trees. He came into view again, and the hard, almost savage look in his pale eyes, was still there.

'Nothing here,' he said grimly. 'Where's Mr. Lowe?'

White explained.

'He seemed uncommonly interested in that bit of mud, Mr. Dene. Dunno what it means, but — '

Together they hurried into the house. If Lowe were on a mysterious trail of his own, they were anxious for further details. But they found him in one of his most uncommunicative moods. He was replacing a book on the shelves in the library as they entered, and glanced at them absently as if barely realising their presence. Without speaking, he dropped into a chair and began refilling his pipe, his eyes fastened on the opposite windows, where the darkening sky could be seen heavy with cloud.

'What's the hunch?' demanded Dene.

Lowe glanced at him rather absently. His thoughts were clearly busy elsewhere. Then he said slowly:

'I fancy that poor devil of a constable has solved our problems for us. The problem of the disappearance of the *Oki Maru*!'

He leant back in his chair, lighting his pipe, once more deep in thought. Dene opened his mouth to put a bewildered question; but he did not speak.

The Secret Service man knew well, and recognised the mood, as did White. They would get nothing out of Lowe until he was ready to give them the results of whatever reasoning his brain was working upon.

Darkness was closing in rapidly round the old house. The wind was increasing, and a spatter of rain whipped the panes of the windows of the gloomy library. The clock on the chimney-piece chimed the hour softly. The rain was falling faster now.

At last with quick abruptness, Lowe rose to his feet. The other two who had been waiting restlessly at the far end of the long room, rose too. Lowe seemed suddenly to realise their presence.

'Wait here!' he said incisively.

He hurried from the room.

'He's on some trail all right!' muttered White. 'Wonder what the devil — '

They heard the front door slam.

Half an hour passed before Lowe returned. He stepped into the library, and stood staring across at them with gleaming eyes, lips compressed. His grey suit was drenched with rain, his hair shining with moisture, and there was thick mud on his shoes. A suppressed excitement rarely seen was revealed in the tense poise of his rain-soaked figure and the queer glitter in his eyes.

'Come along!' he said simply; swung on his heel and vanished from the room.

The front door was standing open, as Dene and Arnold saw as they hurried after the lean figure into the hall.

'What the deuce is in the wind? What do you know?' demanded Dene, his deep voice alive with intense curiosity.

Lowe was striding towards the open door. He swung round at the question. A slow smile touched his lips.

'We're off to hunt for that stolen draft-treaty, that Mlle. Julie got away with so cleverly from the Foreign Office. Both got torches with you? You'll need 'em — it's thundering dark on board the *Oki Maru!*'

15

The Missing Steamer

'On board the *Oki Maru!*' Arnold White echoed Lowe's words in bewildered amazement. 'You mean to say — '

'Exactly!' smiled Lowe. 'I'm taking you on board the *Oki Maru*. The solution to the whole thing came to me — I worked it out from all angles, Dene — '

His eyes had switched to the Secret Service man, gazing back at him with as great astonishment as White.

'I worked it out from all angles,' Lowe repeated, with a shrug. 'And that poor devil of a police-sergeant gave me the clue that made everything clear, once I had hit on the solution. I went and saw if my deductions were correct. They are!'

'The *Oki Maru!* But where — '

'Follow me!'

He swung towards the open door, and hurried down the steps into the dark, rain-swept garden. The strengthening gale was roaring across the grounds from the sea as they followed the hatless figure, head down to the storm, towards the path that led to the gate opening on the cliffs.

Amazing though Lowe's claim seemed, they knew him too well to doubt its authenticity for an instant. For the moment, with Lowe in his uncommunicative mood, Dene could only wonder, inwardly as bewildered as Arnold himself, even though the rugged face of the big-boned Secret Service man betrayed now nothing of his wondering amazement as they passed along the dark path in the teeth of the wind and rain.

But to Dene's surprise, in another twenty yards, Lowe swung aside, following another path. They were not, then, making for the cliffs, and the sea, it seemed, after all!

Lowe left the path and made his way across a stretch of dark, sodden lawn. They saw now that he was heading towards a high-grown shrubbery that separated the kitchen garden from the rest of the grounds.

Under the towering wall of shrubs, Lowe paused, glancing round.

'This way!' he said. 'And have your guns ready!'

He vanished between two tall rhododendrons, and they followed into the pitch blackness beyond.

Lowe's electric torch stabbed the darkness, revealing the dry ground to which the rain had not penetrated, although it was dripping noisily in the leaves above them. He led the way into the heart of the shrubbery, his feet soundless on the soft earth, his lean frame invisible — only the dancing will-o'-the-wisp of the detective's torch to guide them. They came up with him as he halted in a tiny clearing among the great bushes, his torchlight directed to the earth at his feet.

'Here we are,' murmured Lowe.

Dene and Arnold peered round. Too dark for anything to be seen.

'Well?' muttered Dene. 'Damned if I see — '

'Remember that fellow you ran into in the dark, here in these grounds, before you and I accidentally got to grips?' broke in Lowe softly. 'You told us someone had rushed you in the dark, but got away. You thought it was me, back again — '

'I remember,' nodded Dene. 'Moncrieff's murderer!'

'No. Not Moncrieff's murderer. But the murderer, tonight, of Sergeant Owen. When I realised what I had to look for to solve the mystery of the *Oki Maru*, I worked out the direction taken in his flight on each occasion by this elusive individual. He was a different side of the house tonight, but we know the direction he took. I was able to judge, roughly, the direction he took after he escaped you that other time, from what you had told us and the known position of Richards and his men. It was evident to me that he was making for this corner of the grounds on each occasion.

'Why? It leads nowhere. Had he fled to the cliffs, or to the gates, it would have been understandable. But this was his definite line of retreat. Having come to the conclusions I had, I was not surprised. I came out and searched — here. This is what I found — as I had expected to find — '

He raised the beam of his torch. It shot through the darkness into a shadowy space between two of the close-grown bushes, and they saw that a pile of dead rhododendron branches lay there, withered and dead.

'Those dead branches?' muttered Arnold in bewilderment.

'No!' rapped Lowe. 'But what they hide!'

Laying his torch on the ground, he dragged the heap of branches aside. There was an ejaculation from White as he saw a narrow hole in the earth, more than wide enough for a man to squeeze through.

'This is the way,' said Lowe, in a matter-of-fact tone that somehow checked the excited question on Arnold's lips. 'You'll want your torches here.'

He stooped over the yawning opening in the earth and swung down, dropping from sight. They heard his feet strike stone.

Dene leant over the hole and flashed in his torch. He saw that Lowe was crouching by the entrance to a narrow tunnel that led away into the earth, with what looked like three ancient stone steps at the commencement of it.

The dramatist made his way into the tunnel, his tall frame bent double. Dene dropped to the entrance of it, and followed, White coming behind him.

Almost instantly the tunnel widened. Though near the entrance the floor was strewn with trampled earth, beyond they were passing through solid rock — a man-made tunnel that sloped steeply down, with occasional rock steps, and widened in another twenty yards to a natural fissure in the rock, where it was possible for them to walk upright. The air was intensely cold.

It occurred to Dene that, since they had left no clue to their whereabouts with the servants at the house, when Inspector Williams arrived from Caermawr, in response to their telephone call acquainting him with the murder of Sergeant Owen, the police officer would probably be a good deal bewildered to know what had happened to them.

Sometimes narrowing, sometimes widening again, the natural tunnel ran on interminably, as it seemed to the pair following

Lowe. Sometimes it was level, sometimes it even sloped up a little; but as a rule it dropped lower and lower, occasionally with a gradient so steep that unknown hands — evidently of some past generation — had hewn rough steps in the rocky floor.

Its direction, too, despite occasional twists and turns, was on the whole astonishingly straight. With an inward calculation, Dene saw that they were making in the direction of the sea.

'That's so,' nodded Lowe, when Dene voiced this fact. He did not glance round.

'You mean to say that this leads out to the sea, at a spot where the *Oki Maru* sank, close to the cliffs?'

'The *Oki Maru* never sank,' came the cryptic answer.

They turned a corner in the suddenly spacious and lofty tunnel. In a few yards Lowe halted.

'Not another foot!' he ordered sharply. 'Or you're dead men!'

His voice echoed strangely, as if in a vast place. And Dene and Arnold moving wonderingly to Lowe's side, understood why.

Turning the last stretch of the abrupt

bend in the tunnel, a dim, shadowy light had met their eyes, flooding down from somewhere high above their heads. They saw that Lowe was standing on a rock-ledge overlooking a vast natural cavern, and that the light filtered down through a great split in the rocky roof through which a thin stretch of star-spangled sky could be seen; evidently the gale had swept the clouds away, leaving the world outside bathed in starlight, enough penetrating through the natural fissure in the roof of the great cavern to reveal dimly the damp, jagged walls and the lake of still, black water that covered the floor, from which massed boulders rose like crouching animal shapes.

Lowe had snapped out his torch, was staring across at the far end of the cavern. They followed the direction of his eyes, and White's mouth opened dumbly.

'By the great Pete!' breathed Michael Dene.

Protruding from the wall itself was the forepart of a ship, upright, the squat bows appearing to ride the waters of the cavern floor as serenely as though afloat upon them. There was the blunt forecastle, perfectly intact, her anchors hung in place as if ready to get under way; the hatch of her number one hold, properly battened down, her foremast rising unharmed, a shadowy stem, to the lofty roof above. The fore part of the bridge deck was intact, though littered with fallen rock that had smashed the flying-bridge here and there. And then, beyond, nothing of her — a blank wall of earth and tumbled stone that engulfed the rest of the ship as cleanly as though she were a toy vessel that had steamed half-through a paper hoop.

And now, with their eyes growing used to the faint light, they could see upon her bows, beneath the Japanese characters that also spelt her name, in big, white, Roman lettering the name of this lost, silent ship:

OKI MARU

It was Arnold White who broke the tense silence, as they stood peering down through the shadows at the dark vessel whose disappearance on that long-ago night of storm had bewildered so many others as well as themselves.

'Great Scott!' muttered White. 'How the deuce did she get there?'

'Landslide,' answered Lowe tersely. 'Her wireless aerial carried away, interrupting her SOS — her crew taken to the boats, swamped and drowned — a drifting derelict, borne before the storm under these cliffs, half into this great cavern, wedged on the rocks; and then, landslide! That huge landslide of which the dead sergeant told us, Dene! A vast wall of cliff, sliding down upon her, the result, no doubt, of that same storm — bottling her up for all time in this cavern, her after parts embedded in the fall! There she is. She's puzzled us! But there she is — the *Oki Maru!*'

In silence they stared down at the shadowy steamer. There was something oddly awe-inspiring in the sight of that half-ship protruding from the wall of the cavern, so upright and seemingly unharmed, yet lost for ever to the world-wide seas that she had sailed before being buried in this strange grave.

Dene gripped Lowe's arm.

'How did you know? How did you find her? You're a wizard, man — '

'I wouldn't say that!' murmured Lowe, smiling. 'I put two and two together, and at last I managed to make four, where previously I had only been able to make three! As I say, it was the police-sergeant speaking of a big landslide just opposite the house that gave me the real clue. It was certain that the *Oki Maru* could not be at sea. And yet it took me quite a while, oddly enough, to come to the obvious deduction that therefore she must be on land! A cavern in the cliffs, where she would go unfound — yet that seemed unlikely, with this coast alive with fishing-vessels. Then, when I heard of the landslide, as soon as I began once more to go over the mystery, the answer came to me. The *Oki Maru* had been washed into one of the great caverns that split these cliffs, and the landslide had shut her in!

'Of course, it is well known hereabouts that there is a big cavern almost under

Moncrieff's house, towards the sea, and that the recent landslide has closed the entrance. But no one connected that fact with the mysterious disappearance of a certain Japanese steamer!' he concluded dryly.

'Needed you to think of that!' growled Dene.

'Finding that bit of oletonian mud by the dead sergeant made me think — hard!' explained Lowe. 'That kind of subsoil is only to be found hereabouts a certain distance below the upper surface. It could only have come from the murderer's boot — and he had clearly been underground! It all came to me then. I asked old Hurst, the butler, if a cavern had been closed in by the landslide, and he wondered how I guessed it! But, of course, he knew of it — all the local people know of the shut-in cavern, without thinking anything much about it, of course.'

'But someone else knows where the *Oki Maru* is!' muttered Dene. 'The chronometer, and the skipper's watch that must also have been taken off her — '

'Ni!' breathed White. 'Ni knows!'

Lowe shook his head.

'Ni doesn't know — yet! He knows she's in this cave, which is why he's so infernally interested in this house, but he doesn't know the way in, or he wouldn't have had to waste time with anything else! Julie doesn't know, either. But somehow — probably through shadowing Ni or one of his agents — she got wise to the fact that Ni, in his search for the *Oki Maru*, was concentrating on this house. So she waded in cleverly and bought the place, when she found out before Ni that it was for sale.'

'Then who in the world — ' began White.

'Who does know? Who rifled that chronometer and the watch out of her captain's cabin?' Lowe stood gazing down at the shadowy shape of the embedded ship. 'Someone who had not gone off with the rest of the crew in the boats, but had been on board, and escaped with his life as a consequence, when she came to rest down there! Ni's agent on board her; the man from Tokio whom Ni had sent on board as second mate, and who murdered the real second mate, K'Yung, in the

London-Liverpool express, to enable him to take K'Yung's place, as we already know. It could only be that same man — or, otherwise, who had told Ni what had happened to the *Oki Maru*?'

Lowe was again speaking in purely matter-of-fact tones, as he explained the reasoning that had led him to the discovery of the lost ship underground; for the moment, the case had assumed for him an entirely academic interest — a question of fact and deduction, rather than an affair in which three human lives — those of K'Yung, the second mate of the *Oki Maru*, Sir Matthew Moncrieff, and Sergeant Owen of the Caermawr police, had been cold-bloodedly sacrificed by murderous hands.

'Once I realised where the *Oki Maru* was to be found, I asked myself how Ni knew she was there — yet had not succeeded in penetrating to her. Obviously someone else had been aboard her since her disappearance, for that chronometer to have turned up. The only solution to cover both these problems was that Ni's agent, the murderer of K'Yung, had been on board the ship when she was bottled up, that he had found a way out of the cavern, and had somehow been able to communicate with Ni, telling him what had occurred, but without having explained to Ni where the remaining entrance to the cavern was, and that as yet, for one reason or another, Ni had not succeeded in getting into personal contact with the man.

'It was reasonable to assume that this man, living still on the bottled-up ship, as he could of course do, with access to the ship's stores, was the mysterious figure that had so frightened Letitia Delmar, by prowling round the house at night, and even on one occasion at least making his way into the house and being seen by her in the long gallery. His motive for this may have been almost anything — possibly in search of fresh water. He entered the house again later — the night I came — and he had the nasty shock of running into you, Dene, in the plantation. But he managed to elude you and get back to his hiding-place, the cavern where the *Oki Maru* was lying — getting in, of course, by that hole that he himself had scratched through to the surface from the end of that tunnel that runs up to that spot. From the look of it, I should say that the tunnel is a relic of the old smuggling days. The entrance to it had evidently been blocked for years by fallen earth, and forgotten. But, as I say, he scratched his way out. If he hadn't found that means of getting out he would have died down here like a rat in a trap, sooner or later — for nothing but a lizard could hope to climb out that way!'

Lowe pointed as he spoke to the great fissure in the roof through which the starlight fell.

'Yes, lucky for him he found that old smugglers' tunnel!' he went on. 'And he hid the hole he had made pretty cleverly — because he dared not make himself known. When Moncrieff's dogs gave him trouble on his nightly prowls he laid poison for them. There must have been rat-poison ready to hand in the ship.'

'But the chronometer, sold at Birkenhead — ' White's voice was puzzled.

'He wanted money for some reason,'

explained Lowe with a shrug. 'Evidently he had none — possibly his own cabin, with his money, had been buried beneath the landslide! So he collected whatever was saleable on board the ship, including the captain's watch, by the way — found, no doubt, in the captain's cabin, and which he carelessly dropped in the grounds, where you found it. Probably by bribing a lorry-driver with some similar article of value, he got to Birkenhead, about the nearest town where he would be likely to sell the chronometer, as he knew, being a sailor. He made the sale, as we know — and it was reported to Scotland Yard. Why he wanted the money so urgently to go to all that trouble to get it is doubtful. Possibly he intended to go to London to see Ni, and for some reason changed his plans afterwards and returned here to continue his search on board the ship for the treaty it was his task to get hold of. For that, certainly, must still be on board!'

'Then it was he who knifed Richards on the roof, and got away to Ni's yacht?' muttered White.

Lowe shook his head.

'No. That must have been another of Ni's men, who had been sent to spy out the land, at the same time that Ni himself coolly presented himself at the front door with a bluff of wishing to buy the house. At least, not bluff — if Julie hadn't forestalled him, he would no doubt have been only too glad to buy it, in the circumstances! But he thought it wisest to clear off promptly when he found the place in the hands of the police, with Moncrieff murdered. He must have guessed immediately that Moncrieff had been knifed by one of his own men.

'Yes, there were two of Ni's satellites on the prowl — a man from the yacht which was waiting in the cove, and the actual man from the *Oki Maru!* And neither can have known of the other's presence or whereabouts! Of course, at the time we naturally assumed that both were one and the same man. But it was the man from Tokio that ran into you in the plantation, Dene, and the man from the yacht who murdered Moncrieff and later scrawled that message in Japanese — to scare us

— and was finally hunted from the roofs after he had knifed Richards up there!'

'Then — ' Dene's queerly glimmering eyes were riveted on the half-obliterated ship. 'Then he's still on board her, that feller that murdered K'Yung! The bogus second mate — '

'Oh, yes, he is still on board,' murmured Lowe casually. 'And, since he usually only comes out at night, we can feel certain he is on board at this very moment. So, too, is that treaty you want, Dene! Or he would have cleared off with it — immediately he found it! To take it to Ni.'

'Look!' breathed Arnold swiftly.

Even as Lowe had finished speaking, a distant figure had appeared on the shadowy foredeck of the imprisoned ship — a figure dim and vague enough, though the big ship's lantern that he carried made a bright point of swaying light in the gloom.

Across the vast cavern, their voices had been inaudible to the man on board the lost steamer, it was evident enough, for he clearly had no suspicion of their presence

268

as he crossed the dark deck.

Three pairs of eyes watched him from the high-up ledge.

'There goes the man whom Scotland Yard want for the murder of the unidentified Korean who was really the second mate of the *Oki Maru!*' said Lowe quietly. 'We've got him like a rat in a trap — '

The man passing along the foredeck of the *Oki Maru* could be seen now to be carrying something over his shoulder — a spade or pick.

He reached the bridge-deck, the lantern swaying up the starboard ladder. At the top, by the end of the alleyway that ran — once — through to the after-deck, though blocked now by the landslide that had crushed the after-part of the bridge-deck down upon it, the distant, tiny figure set down the lantern. They heard, faint in the grave-like silence of the cave, the clink of a pick.

'He's clearing a way through into the ship!' muttered White.

'Been working at that day after day, we can be sure!' nodded Lowe. 'It's that treaty that he wants, and he may have a pretty good idea where it is — if he can only get to it!'

With fascinated eyes they watched the labouring figure clearing away the mass of tumbled earth and stone that blocked the mouth of the starboard alleyway. Their eyes had grown so used to the faint light that filtered down into the great cave that they could see him working fairly clearly, aided by the glow of the lantern. There was something almost eerie in that shadowy figure working there in this cold cavern that was the tomb of the *Oki Maru*.

'Come on!' muttered Lowe. 'Not a sound!'

A steep, rocky path, interspersed with rough-hewn steps, led down from the ledge on which they stood to the floor of the cave. Lowe had thrust his torch back into his pocket, and by the faint light from above made his way noiselessly down the treacherous slope. Dene and Arnold followed — three shadows, all but invisible against the dark, rocky wall to which the pathway clung, stealing down to the ship below.

The man on board the trapped steamer

was still utterly unconscious that he was not alone. The faint sounds of his labours continued steadily. At last Lowe and his companions had arrived on the shelving rocks that edged the dark, imprisoned lake of sea-water that lay like a sheet of ebony around the ship.

A natural causeway of rocks ran out to the dark hull — evidently the means by which the sole survivor of the lost ship reached the pathway by which they had descended, for they could see now that a ship's ladder dangled over the side of the *Oki Maru* at the point where the line of rocks reached her.

Gathered in the shadow, the three peered across towards the steamer. Now that they were on the water's edge, the bows of the *Oki Maru* seemed weirdly huge in the faint light, towering high above them. The noise of the pick had ceased. And now, abruptly, they saw the lantern sway again, vanish from sight into the narrow alleyway that ran under the lofty bridge-deck.

'He's cleared a way through!' breathed Arnold White.

It was Dene who led the way quickly out on to the flat boulders that formed a natural pathway out to the ship. Moving lithely from rock to rock, the big figure of the Secret Service man made its way swiftly across, and Lowe and White followed noiselessly. Once Arnold missed his footing on a slippery boulder, and all but fell — but he regained his balance in the nick of time, and hurried on.

Dene reached the towering hull, gripped the wooden rungs of the dangling rope-ladder, and swung himself upwards. A minute later all three of them were crouching on the shadowy deck of the silent ship.

On board the *Oki Maru!* A queer thrill in that thought, Arnold told himself. This mystery ship that had been lost so strangely, which no human eye had expected ever to see again!

Lowe and Dene were peering aft.

A glimmer of light was visible through one of the port-holes that overlooked the foredeck.

'He's got into the cabin there!' murmured the dramatist. 'The first mate's cabin, probably. Perhaps he knows that it was the first mate who had been entrusted with the stolen treaty! If so — '

They stole across the iron plates of the deck. They were red with rust, littered here and there with boulders that had rolled along from the main mass of the landslide in which the after-part of the *Oki Maru* was embedded. Picking their way silently, they reached the iron ladder that led up to the point where the man they had been watching had been toiling to clear a way through to the cabin which he had now gained. Smashed and bent though the ladder was — evidently it had been struck by some falling debris when the landslide had crashed down upon the ship — it was easy enough to negotiate. Lowe swung up it, and a few moments later was crouching on the narrow strip of deck that passed athwart-ships before the wall of the saloon and the flanking officers' cabins.

Dene joined him there, with White.

The lantern-light still glowed out through the port-hole by which they crouched. Lowe rose slowly to his feet and peered in.

A cat-like figure was busy searching through the contents of an overturned metal trunk, his back towards the port-hole — a man who wore the blue reefer coat and stripes of a second-officer, though soiled and torn. And then, as he straightened with a quick, triumphant movement, his face turned so as to become visible.

A yellow-brown face with jet-black eyes, and thin lips twisted now into a grin of exultation, as his lean brown hands ripped open the seals of an oblong paper packet from which he had already torn the string. With feverish excitement revealed in every movement in the glittering black eyes, the man who had sailed as second-mate on board the *Oki Maru* while the real second-mate lay murdered by the gleaming main line rails between Liverpool and London, tore open the bulky packet — revealed the thick typewritten manuscript within.

Lowe drew a deep breath.

The stolen draft-treaty from the Foreign Office!

'He's found it!' he muttered grimly. 'It's yours, Dene — '

The man within the narrow cabin had turned towards the port-hole, and suddenly he froze, as though turned to stone.

The light of the lantern set upon the bunk within the cabin had revealed to him the eyes gazing in upon him. His jaw sagged open, and the papers in his hands fell to the floor of the cabin from shaking, nerveless hands.

To the man from Tokio it seemed like some supernatural face staring in at him through the port-hole, believing as he had that he alone could enter the cavern where the *Oki Maru* lay tombed in the silence. And a shuddering shriek broke from him as he reeled back, hands raised as if to ward off the apparition.

'Get him!' muttered Lowe.

Dene was already stumbling over the loose earth and stones that littered the alleyway to a depth of a foot or more, as he made his way with set jaw towards the door of the cabin in which the terrified Korean crouched back against the wall in a sweat of superstitious terror.

He kicked the door open, and his big figure filled the doorway as he stood surveying the man within, a sardonic smile playing around his strong lips.

'I want those papers!' he growled.

The man from Tokio stared up at him for a moment like a half-stunned man.

Lowe's face had vanished from the port-hole as he hurried to join Dene, and that there were two different men on board with him the Korean did not guess. Already the abrupt realisation had come to him that Dene was a man of flesh and blood. His expression altered with that sudden understanding. With a soundless exclamation, he dragged a knife from his coat and hurled himself at the figure in the doorway.

Swift though Dene was, the knife slashed through his coat and ripped his shoulder before he could ward off the lightning attack. Then the Korean crashed back with a fist under his yellow chin, went down like a sack of potatoes against the bunk, his oblique black eyes closed, his head slumped loosely forward. Dene laughed shortly, and put a hand gingerly to his shoulder. Warm blood flowed to his touch.

'Skewered me, the hound!' he jerked over his shoulder laconically to the others.

They came quickly into the cabin. Dene stooped and picked up the manuscript that lay amid the litter there. A Foreign Office seal was stamped across it, and there was a note attached to it that bore a signature Dene knew well. The signature of Sir Vrymer Fane, Secretary of State for Foreign Affairs.

'It'll take ten years off Fane's age to see this again,' chuckled Dene, thrusting the thick manuscript into his pocket in a careless roll.

'Listen!'

Trevor Lowe had been bending over the knocked-out Korean, and had satisfied himself that his man would soon recover his senses from that hammer-blow of Dene's big fist. But now he rose abruptly, head turned towards the cabin door, listening.

'Didn't hear anything,' muttered White.

'Perhaps it was some debris dropping in the cave.' But Lowe was frowning. 'I certainly heard something. We'd better just make sure — '

He stepped past Dene and made his way out of the cabin and back to the head of the iron ladder leading down to the shadowy fore-deck. They followed him quickly, Dene shutting and locking the cabin door.

They peered into the gloom. A faint whisper of sound among the shadows on the rusted iron deck came to their ears, and guns appeared simultaneously in their hands.

The next instant the blaze of a powerful electric lamp flamed out of the darkness, revealing the three of them in a frozen group where they stood by the twisted ladder. It was directed upon them from the deck below, blinding white, blotting out all else in the wall of blackness beyond.

'I must ask you to drop those guns, my dear sirs!'

A soft, caressing voice addressed them from somewhere beyond the blaze of powerful electric lamp-light.

'You will obey my instructions if you

are wise men,' went on the voice softly. 'You are covered by seven guns at this moment, and you make an excellent target.'

The voice of Ni, alive with hideous triumph.

With an ejaculation, Michael Dene whipped up his gun and aimed at the spot from which the voice seemed to come.

Next moment a bullet grazed his arm.

'You see?' came the derisive voice of Ni. 'A great mistake, Mr. Dene! I fear you are possessed of a reckless temperament, as I have previously discovered. And yet I warned you.'

For a second or two the light left them, swung sideways and round, to reveal a knot of men gathered on the deck of the grounded ship — each with a dark automatic raised towards them. The light swept back upon them almost instantly, but not before Dene and Arnold had recognised some of those faces. Two yellow men and five whites. Part of the crew of the *Sea Witch*!

That they had approached and boarded the ship so silently was not surprising, for each of them, they had had time to notice, wore the rubber-soled canvas shoes used by yacht-hands.

'Raise your arms!'

The command out of the darkness was in a different tone. The soft, evil caressiveness had changed to a malignant snarl.

For a moment or two Lowe hesitated. Then he realised the uselessness of defying that order. Despite the gun in his hand, he could see nothing of their enemies, with that blaze of light flooding direct upon his eyes. A lucky shot might wound, or even kill, one of them, but there were still the others, all armed, and with himself forming a childishly easy target, revealed as he was in the glare of white light from the electric lamp on the deck below.

Slowly he raised his arms, and White followed suit. Dene left his right arm hanging limply at his side. It was doubly wounded now, a useless thing, with that knife-gash in the shoulder and the numbed forearm from the bullet wound there.

'Throw down your weapons!'

Useless to defy the order! Lowe and Arnold tossed their weapons over the rail; Dene's had already fallen.

'You are wise!' There was a soft, hideous laugh from the darkness. Ni's voice was mocking, complacent, as he added blandly: 'So! You found the *Oki Maru*, gentlemen!'

'We found it,' said Dene laconically.

'Unfortunately for you, so have I,' murmured the voice of Ni. 'And now, you will observe, you are in my hands.'

'I've observed it,' agreed Dene.

There was a sound behind them in the alleyway.

The man from Tokio whom Dene had put to sleep had recovered his senses. He had heard voices and seen through the port-hole what the situation was. Now he came staggering into view, still partly dazed, but with a light of evil joy in his yellow-brown face.

He came into the range of light, and Lowe heard a hissing indrawn breath that he took to come from Ni.

There was a swift torrent of unintelligible Korean in Ni's voice, answered by the eagerly gesticulating man near them. The two who had been comrades years ago in Tokio, exchanged swift question and answer; and then Ni gave a gloating laugh, and spoke once more in English.

'My servant tells me that he has found those certain papers for which we have all, I understand, been looking,' he purred. 'And that you, Mr. Dene, at the moment have those papers in your possession.'

'That's exactly right,' said Dene.

'Ah! You will now, I fear, have the great disappointment of having to deliver those papers to me,' came the complacent, triumphant voice of Ni. 'Kindly descend, Mr. Dene, down that ladder. You other two remain where you are. And you will please remember to keep your arms nicely raised.'

Dene did not move. His pale blue eyes were gleaming queerly. They heard the shuffle of feet on the deck below as one of Ni's satellites stirred restlessly where he stood covering the three.

'And suppose I don't!' he asked. 'What then, Ni?'

'Then of course you die!' Ni's voice

was baleful. 'You die with several bullets in your body, and the papers are taken from your pocket just the same. Reckless though you are by nature, I don't take you for a fool, Mr. Dene.'

'You flatter me,' drawled Michael Dene. 'But I agree I'm not fool enough to order my own funeral. I'll come.'

He moved slowly to the ladder, and descended to the deck beneath.

There was a queer, twisted grin on his rugged face as he paused, one hand in his pocket, revealed vividly in the blaze of the powerful electric lamp that revealed both them and him in its wide circular beam.

'Not pleasant being made to surrender up one's country's secrets, Ni,' he said grimly. 'Britain's secrets — to a yellow-skinned snake like you!'

'A ready gun can make most men traitors,' mocked Ni.

'That's an ugly word, traitor,' said Dene, harshly. 'Still — '

He moved slowly forward.

'Here you are, Ni,' he grated, and held out the rolled manuscript, stamped with the Foreign Office seal.

The stout figure of Ni stepped swiftly forward into the range of lamp-light — the lamp was held by one of his men, it appeared. The round, smooth yellow-brown face of the Korean millionaire was perfectly unemotional, despite the gloating inward triumph Dene knew the man must feel. There was a quiet, bland smile on Ni's lips as he took the papers, glanced at them coolly, and thrust them into his own pocket.

'Thank you, Mr. Dene,' murmured Mr. Tsu Ni. 'A thousand thanks! I never thought to receive this great prize, when I finally obtained it, from the hands of a British Secret Service man in person. I am most sensitive of the honour, Mr. Dene.'

'Then you know who I am?'

'But of course!' Ni waved a plump, yellow hand. 'Who has not heard of the famous Michael Dene — even though few have knowingly seen him?' He bowed derisively, his black eyes snakelike with a momentary glitter. 'I am deeply honoured indeed.'

284

'That's grand,' drawled Dene.

Ni stepped back into the darkness behind the unwavering glare of light. He spoke swiftly, and two of the crew of the *Sea Witch* moved quickly forward and gripped Dene on either side. Lowe and White, watching from above, saw Dene stiffen as if to resist; then the Secret Service man seemed to realise the uselessness of so doing. He shrugged his sound shoulder, and let himself be held. His arms were dragged behind his back and bound, and they saw him wince as his wounded arm was jerked backwards.

'Now you two there, kindly come down! You are well covered, remember!'

They had no choice but to obey.

A minute later they were standing bound with Dene by the base of the soaring, shadowy mast. The powerful lamp had been hung on the iron bulwark, revealing now all those on the deck — Ni and his seven men from the yacht, together with the three captives and the man who had been second mate of the *Oki Maru*.

The latter was chattering excitedly to

Ni, who was answering quickly. It was evident that the two were giving mutual explanations; and from the fawning manner of the murderer of K'Yung it was clear that he feared his master. Ni turned at last to his prisoners, smiling blandly. Before he could speak, Lowe put a quiet question that brought a look of sheer astonishment to Ni's beady eyes.

'Why did that man of yours sell that chronometer in Birkenhead, Ni?'

'How did you know of that?' demanded Ni, amazed.

Lowe shrugged.

'I know quite a lot — though I don't know the reason for his doing that. From a purely academic point of view I should be interested to learn the reason.'

Ni was clearly puzzled by this evidence of Lowe's knowledge — a mysterious knowledge, it seemed to Ni. But he shrugged blandly.

'To enable him to obtain money to come to London,' he explained, in a derisive tone. 'This man was on board the *Oki Maru*, my agent,' he added, blandly boastful. 'A clever move on my part, was it not, after I had discovered that the stolen treaty had been placed in charge of the first mate of this ship? A French Secret Service vessel was to wait for her on the line of her route, and pick up the treaty from a waterproof floating case in which it was to be dropped for them. I intended to interfere with that plan. I, too, was waiting along the route of the *Oki Maru*, in my yacht. I was going to pick up that treaty, when it was dropped for me by my agent, before the ship reached the spot where the French vessel would be waiting. I had no doubt that my agent would succeed in stealing it from the first officer's cabin. He is a clever man, is Puhm!'

'I see!' The dramatist was genuinely interested, despite their position as prisoners of this cold-blooded scoundrel, who most probably contemplated taking their lives in order to silence them for ever, so that he might once more resume his position in London life. 'I see! But the storm upset your plans.'

'Naturally,' nodded Ni. He seemed proud of his boasted cleverness, to enjoy explaining his moves and counter-moves. 'Puhm did not leave the ship, however, with the rest of them. He knew it would go ill with him to leave that ship without the treaty I had ordered him to find. And that saved his life, though trapping him in this cave. He could not, after finding his way out, write to me direct, as he knew me to be at sea in the *Sea Witch*. He wrote, however, to an English colleague of mine in London, whose address he had in English, which he could copy, though ignorant of English. He wrote in Japanese. Since my English colleague, on the other hand, could not read or understand Japanese or Korean, Puhm copied the name of the ship in English lettering from the name on the bows to show my friend in London what the letter concerned, so that my friend would understand and forward the letter to me as soon as possible — '

'Jove!' muttered Dene. 'I understand!'

He was thinking of that letter that he had obtained from their guard at the lonely ruined cottage on the cliffs, and which Julie had robbed him of later. He knew now what that letter had been.

'Unfortunately,' pursued Ni, in the same bland tones, 'Puhm's letter, though informing me when I eventually received it, of the fate of the *Oki Maru*, and his hope of being able to dig his way through to the cabin where he knew the treaty to be hidden, he was unable to tell me the whereabouts of the cave. Though he had penetrated to the house above, he knew no English, and, in any case, dared not make inquiries locally as to the name of the district. All he could do in his letter was to describe as minutely as possible the aspect of the coastline, and so on, and leave me to find it as best I could. This, of course, I eventually did, though unfortunately only after considerable delay. And, meanwhile, since I failed to come, Puhm imagined I had failed to receive his letter, and determined to go to London in search of me, thinking I must be back there. So he collected one or two valuable articles, managed to get to Birkenhead by road, sold the chronometer and one or two other articles, and took the train to London. There he found I was at sea, searching for the spot where the *Oki Maru* had been sealed up, so of course he returned here. By an unfortunate mischance our clever and charming young friend, Mlle Julie, of the French Secret Service, saw him in London, knew who he was, and followed him here. So I learnt from the lady herself after my brief capture of her delightful person. She did not, however, see him take to earth — most fortunately for my ambitions to obtain possession of this document.'

He tapped his breast-pocket, where the rolled manuscript bulged, and glanced smilingly from Dene to the other two.

'Naturally,' he went on, 'as soon as my cruising along this coast brought me to the spot I recognised from Puhm's letter as being the spot where the landslide had occurred, I set to work to seek out the hidden entrance to the cavern. Unfortunately, I only knew that it was near the house which Puhm had described. So I came first to the house — you remember my arrival, gentlemen? But I failed to come across my faithful Puhm. So I was still unable to go down to the ship I knew to lie sealed somewhere beneath my feet. In fact, I saw nothing of Puhm until a few minutes ago on board this ship. But I did discover — or one of my men did — the hole in the ground by which you yourselves had entered. I was seeking for it tirelessly, of course, and eventually my patience was rewarded. Unfortunate for you gentlemen, was it not?'

Arnold White's face changed.

It came to him in a flash that he had forgotten, in his eagerness, to drag back the concealing branches over the narrow hole in the shrubbery when following Lowe and Dene, though, as the last to enter, they had assumed that he would do so.

His fault that Ni had found that entrance! His fault that they were prisoners in Ni's hands, with the precious treaty also in Ni's gloating possession!

He jerked out his confession.

'Can't be helped, Arnold,' said Lowe quietly.

'What now, Ni?' demanded Dene. 'You've talked a lot — but what are you going to *do*?'

Ni drew from his pocket his long cigarette-holder, smilingly inserted a cigarette, and lit it with stout, evil suavity.

'I regret to say, gentlemen,' he purred, 'that I am going to leave you here — dead.'

16

Julie's Triumph

In the tense silence that filled the great dim-lit cavern, the words, so suavely spoken, seemed to echo in the vast shadowy spaces like the knell of doom.

'After that,' grinned the Korean, 'I shall, of course, close up the entrance.' He gestured with a fat, yellow hand towards the pathway that led up the side of the cavern to the old smugglers' tunnel. 'Your bodies will be sealed up with the ship — perhaps for ever. If this cavern should ever be found, on the other hand, it will make, no doubt, a most interesting newspaper story at some distant date, the story of a lost ship found at last, with three human skeletons rotting on her deck!'

'You've got a picturesque way of putting it, Ni,' said Dene evenly.

But despite the coolness of his words

his eyes were lit by an ugly light as he stared into the snake-like eyes of the Eastern millionaire.

Lowe, standing there bound at his side, betrayed nothing of his inner feelings, whatever they may have been, as he, too, surveyed Ni coolly enough.

His eyes went from face to face — from Ni's smooth, smiling one to the malignant ones of the crew of the *Sea Witch*.

White men, for the most part — that, at any rate, the colour of their skins. But from these sweepings of some Continental port, there was no help.

White was no coward. He had proved that fact a hundred times during his association with Lowe. But despite himself he felt his heart go suddenly cold, as he stared round at that ring of evil, murderous faces. Their death-warrant was signed and sealed; that could be read in any of those malevolent eyes bent upon them.

Not that he was himself afraid of death, strong though the natural desire for life was within him. It was the knowledge that it had been his own oversight in failing to drag back the concealing branches above the entrance to this underground cavern that had been the cause of their being captured down here like rats in a trap, which appalled him.

Thanks to that oversight he had helped to encompass the deaths of the others!

He licked his lips, which had gone suddenly dry.

'You dirty yellow snake, Ni!' muttered Dene.

The bland smiling suavity on Ni's face, as the Korean drew almost daintily at the long cigarette-holder between his brown lips, died away. His face went malignant, devilish, as he stepped forward and struck the Secret Service man across the face.

'So!' he said viciously. 'Your deaths shall not be pleasant! You shall die neither by the knife nor the gun!'

He flung a pointing hand to the mast that tapered above their heads.

'You shall hang from that! By your necks — but not so that you strangle! You will be left hanging, alive! You will hear the explosion that will seal the tunnel above you! I have dynamite for that. For a few hours, perhaps, you will remain conscious. No more, certainly. You will have time to remember that I — ' For a moment he seemed to choke. 'That I am a yellow snake!'

He swung towards his followers, rapped out a jerked command.

There was rope in plenty ready to hand.

'You yellow snake!' repeated Michael Dene evenly.

The smile had returned to Ni's lips as he stood, fat and evil, watching the ropes knotted round the necks of his three captives — knotted so that the nooses should not tighten when they were dragged on high.

'The mysterious disappearance of Mr. Trevor Lowe, the famous dramatist, will cause excitement in your country!' purred Ni. 'And the disappearance of Mr. Michael Dene, the great Secret Service man, will dismay the Foreign Office! I wonder if your bodies will ever be found? I think not — I think not!'

He dragged from his pocket the rolled documents, and shook them with exultant triumph in their faces.

'There is a last thought for you! That I have this!' He panted out the words. 'I have your country's secret papers! I — '

From somewhere across the dark lake of water surrounding the bows of the ship, a point of fire winked for a second like a crimson eye.

An echoing report rang from wall to wall, and one of the white sailors standing, grinning, at Ni's side, staggered with a sobbing cry, toppled forward on to his face at Ni's feet, and lay writhing.

Ni stood staring down at the fallen man in stupefaction.

A second report, echoing across the vast cavern — and the man knotting the rope round Arnold White's neck staggered sideways, with blood spurting from his cheek where the bullet had grazed.

The two shots had come from the side of the cave opposite to that where the narrow pathway wound up the rock wall to the tunnel that gave entrance.

Silence followed that second shot, as the echoes of it died away — a silence broken only by the moaning of the man at

Ni's feet, and the frightened cursing of the man whose cheek had been hit. A tense, heavy silence — and then a third shot came whining across the dark water, and drilled a clean hole through the crumpled documents in Ni's hand.

Ni leapt sideways, livid-faced, glaring like a madman in the direction from which the shots had come. He snarled a wild order to his men.

But before they could fire in answer at their unseen attackers, half a dozen shots in swift succession came singing across to the deck of the *Oki Maru* from the dark rocks beyond.

Two of Ni's men tottered, and one went down.

Ni was gesticulating, shouting; but this sudden attack, almost eerie in its unexpectedness, had unnerved the six of his satellites who still remained on their feet — two of them damaged even though they had not fallen. There was a panic-rush for the far side of the deck.

'Come back!' snarled Ni. 'Cowards — fools! Shoot — shoot — '

He snatched up the fallen weapons of

one of the men, and blazed into the darkness. The bullet could be heard ricochetting among the rocks. It was answered by two winking jets of flame; and the Korean millionaire, the smoking gun slipping from his fat fingers, sagged silently to the deck across the back of the moaning victim of that first shot — lay still, the rolled manuscript, with its clean-drilled bullet hole, still clasped in his left hand.

His satellites were scrambling wildly down the ladder to the rocks, pounding towards the foot of the climbing path that led to the tunnel. There was a splash as one of them missed his footing as he ran, and vanished into the dark water. He cried out, clawing with slipping fingers at the slimy rocks — then slid back into the depths, and was lost to sight.

Again a bullet whined through the shadows, splintered on the rocks by the foot of the pathway. The scrambling figures gained the path and rushed the slope in wild panic — another bullet crashing against the rocks by their feet. Their shadowy figures vanished above;

and from White's lips there broke a queer crackled laugh.

From high above, by the entrance to the tunnel, they could hear the faint echoing footsteps of the retreating men from the *Sea Witch*. While on the rusted iron deck of the *Oki Maru*, three men lay, one of them groaning at their feet, where they stood with the ropes knotted round their necks, bound and helpless — waiting for what the darkness should reveal.

They had not long to wait.

Two figures appeared on the rocks to their left, making for the causeway that led across to the ship. They were indistinguishable in the shadow. But as they came hurrying towards the ship, drawing swiftly nearer, there was a breathless ejaculation from Dene.

'Julie!'

There was no mistaking now that slender, graceful figure.

With her was the tall, muscular figure of a man.

They heard the wooden rungs of the rope ladder rattle against the iron side of the ship. A lovely face, coolly smiling, rose into view — and Mlle. Julie swung lightly down on to the deck.

There was a gun in her hand. A gun, too, in the hand of the tall Frenchman who followed her.

Dene could guess who the man was. Julie had spoken of having left her car when coming to spy out the land at Moncrieff's house before falling into the hands of Ni's satellites. She would have a subordinate with her, no doubt, in case of emergency, to act as chauffeur meanwhile. This was evidently he.

'Well, mes amis?'

The melodious voice of Mlle. Julie was alive with amusement as she stood surveying the three of them.

'You've saved our bacon, Julie,' said Dene, gruffly.

She laughed gaily, shrugging her slender shoulders.

'You are glad to see me, m'sieurs? And yet, M'sieur Dene, you were not pleased with me last time we met!'

'When you pinched that letter from me?' growled Dene. 'No — I was thundering annoyed with you, m' dear!

But now, for goodness' sake, take this rope off me!'

'Perhaps not yet!' she murmured. Her eyes danced from him to Lowe, from Lowe to White and then back. 'A long time since I have had the pleasure to meet the old friend of mine, the great English dramatist!'

Lowe smiled.

'You've certainly chosen the right time for our meeting, mam'selle!'

Her eyes went back to Dene. Behind her, the tall figure of the Frenchman stood with an expression of lazy indifference on his dark handsome face.

'Yes, M'sieur Dene, you were angry with me, when I stole that letter!' went on Julie amusedly. 'And yet, it was good for you I did, mon vieux! For it told me the truth about this ship — when Leon here translated it for me into French from the Japanese! I knew of the secret way into the cave, although I had no knowledge where it was. But when I saw M'sieur Ni and his cochons disappear in the shrubbery, I was able then to guess! And so down I came, with Leon — and we watched!'

She shrugged again, smiling alluringly in the faint light.

'Just the two of us! Clever of us, no? The way we frightened them away? They thought there were many of us! And we fired from the other side of the cave, so that they could have clear the way of escape!'

She laughed merrily. And then, as her eyes fell on the face of the figure immediately at her feet, she recognised the stout features of Ni himself, she caught her breath.

'C'est lui!' she whispered.

She bent down swiftly, snatching the rolled document from Ni's inert grasp.

Hastily she unrolled it, and her eyes blazed with triumph at sight of the stamped Foreign Office seal. She scanned the typewritten sheet, and turned swiftly to her companion, an excited torrent of French breaking from her.

Leon took the document and thrust it into his pocket. His air of lazy indifference had vanished in a flash. He turned a look of joyous triumph to Lowe and Dene.

'So!' he cried exultantly. 'Mam'selle wins!'

'Mademoiselle wins!' agreed Dene wearily.

Julie was bending again over Ni.

'He still lives,' she said quietly, as she rose again. 'He will recover.'

The man who had been groaning was quiet now. He, too, was senseless. But the third man, a Korean, whom one of Leon's bullets had taken full in the heart, had died before he fell.

Julie stood frowning, thoughtful. She glanced at Leon, who muttered something in her ear. It was clear that he was eager to be gone, with their prize.

Julie nodded, and turned again to the three bound men.

'Au revoir, m'sieurs,' she murmured softly. 'I am glad I saved your lives. That was most good — I like you too well to have seen you die without much sorrow! But I must leave you as you are. For otherwise it is, of course, your duty to try to recover that document I want so much, for my government!'

She had turned towards the side of the

ship. Leon was already waiting impatiently by the head of the rope ladder.

'But damn it, Julie — ' broke out Michael Dene.

She interrupted him, with a smiling gesture.

'But, of course, I shall give word to your friends above — the police! I shall inform them at once where you are to be found. But I must make sure of my own escape, you understand. They will come down for you, without a doubt, very soon!'

Gaily she blew a kiss to the three of them, and disappeared lithely down the ladder, followed by the Frenchman.

They watched her hurrying back across the rocks, saw the two shadowy figures scramble up the steep path, to be lost in another minute in the darkness of the ledge from which the tunnel opened.

Dene laughed queerly.

'She's a reckless little soul, if ever there was one!' he breathed. 'Fancy tackling Ni and his crowd almost single-handed! Lord, don't I wish she were in the British Intelligence, instead of working for the Quai D'Orsay!'

'The Quai D'Orsay won't be likely to agree with you,' said Lowe grimly — 'not when she arrives safe back in Paris with that treaty! She saved our lives. We have to be grateful to her for that. But she's got away with the treaty, man!'

A swift ejaculation from Arnold broke in upon his words.

'Great Scott — '

He was wrenching at the cords that bound his arms.

'A bit of luck at last!' he muttered excitedly.

'Hanged if one of those bullets hasn't cut one of these cords — feels like it — '

Even as he spoke, the half-severed cord which one of the flying bullets had grazed, snapped under the pressure he was exerting. He twisted his arms free of the loosened bonds; and in another minute the other two were free men.

The slippery boulders, with their dank, clinging weeds, betrayed their hurrying feet more than once, as the three of them made their way swiftly to the foot of the pathway that led to the exit from the great cavern. But despite their haste, they gained the rocks beyond the water's edge in safety — one thought in the minds of each.

Time yet to overtake Julie in her flight from the entombed ship!

'We'll get that treaty from her, yet!' said Lowe, as he ran scrambling up the narrow, treacherous path. 'She's only a few minutes start of us!'

There was a queer, chuckling laugh from Dene.

At the head of the path, where it twisted into the tunnel that led through the solid rock to the garden of the old house above, White flung a swift glance back.

In the dim cavernous depths below them the great rusted bows of the *Oki Maru* towered huge.

'What about Ni?' he muttered. 'He's alive — '

'Ni won't go away!' rapped Lowe. 'We'll send our friends the police down for Ni!'

A cold, wet wind lashed their faces as they emerged from the tunnel-mouth. Broken moonlight filled the shadowy grounds of the big old house. As they emerged from the shrubbery on to the lawn beyond, Dene flung out a pointing hand.

'Look — '

Two hurrying figures were visible for a moment, down a long avenue of trees to their left; two figures that vanished almost instantly into the darkness at the end of the avenue, but which all three had recognised.

Mademoiselle Julie, and the Frenchman, Leon.

What had caused the delay to the girl spy's get-away, they could not know; but for some reason Julie and her comrade were only a few hundred yards ahead of them. Their luck seemed almost too good to last, as Lowe told himself grimly, breaking into a run in pursuit of the now vanished figures, Dene and White racing at his side.

It was no time to send Arnold to the house to tell the police there of the secret of the cave, and so to ensure Ni's capture! He was needed with them, now that their pursuit of Julie and the Frenchman had become, so unexpectedly, a direct chase.

They plunged into the darkness of the avenue. At the far end a side-gate opened from the grounds into a lane, and as they tore through the open gate, the sound of their pursuing footsteps drowned by the rising wind that tossed the trees, Lowe saw that some little distance along the lane two cars were drawn up among the shadows.

One, the car which the French girl had so cleverly obtained possession of, after their joint escape from the cottage on the cliffs; the other, presumably Julie's own car — a long-bonneted closed saloon, that was already moving slowly forward with a soft purr of powerful engines.

Lowe whipped from his pocket the automatic that he had snatched up from the deck of the *Oki Maru* before leaving the entombed vessel. A gash of flame tongued-out from the levelled weapon.

But as he had pressed the trigger the moving car had leapt forward with sudden swift acceleration, as though those within had realised their presence. The bullet scattered the loose stones less than a foot behind the near-side rear wheel, harmlessly. And the dark car, with a rapidly rising roar from its exhaust, leapt away like a live thing, vanishing round the bend of the lane.

'They saw us!' panted White.

'They saw us all right!' agreed Lowe. 'And with Julie driving that car it's going to be a hell-for-leather chase, if ever there was one!'

Already the three of them were racing towards the second car.

Lowe himself slid in behind the driving-wheel, Dene at his side, and Arnold scrambled in behind. A touch on the self-starter, and the engines hummed to life.

'Thank heaven they didn't bother to put her out of action!' growled Dene. 'They would have had a shot at it, anyway, if they'd guessed there was any chance of us being hot on their heels! Our luck's holding!' he added jerkily, with a dry chuckle.

'It'll need to hold, if we're to get that treaty back from Julie!' Lowe's voice was hard.

'Once Julie gets her pretty little hands on a thing, it's not child's play to prise it out of them — that's my experience!'

'Mine, too!' nodded Dene, and for a moment an odd twisted smile touched the Secret Service man's lips.

With Lowe's foot jammed hard down on the accelerator, the car swept round the bend of the lane.

Already they were travelling at a reckless, breakneck speed.

So, evidently, was the car ahead. The stretch of lane ahead of them was empty to the next bend. But as they swept round the second twist in the lane, the branches of the overgrown hedges on either side scraping their windows savagely, a point of ruby light came abruptly into view.

The tail-light of Julie's car — travelling at a mad pace.

Again it vanished. But the next bend of the lane led them out on to the wider road beyond. With a slashing backwheel skid, they took the main road, barely three hundred yards behind their quarry.

A spurt of flame winked back at them from the racing machine in front of them, and a bullet struck one of their mudguards and ricochetted away over the road.

'That's one from Leon!' snarled Dene, and half-raised his own weapon. His wounded arm hurt him, but he could use it now without much difficulty.

Dene, like Lowe, had brought his present weapon from the *Oki Maru*. But though he had levelled it at the car ahead, arm thrust out through the open window at his side, elbow resting on the woodwork, he did not fire. He withdrew his arm with a rueful grin.

'I can't take a pot at 'em — not with Julie on board!' he growled. 'A burst tyre at that speed might kill them both; and I don't want a woman's death on my hands! Not Julie's in particular! She's a likeable little cat!'

No second shot had come from the leading car.

'They're short of shells!' muttered Lowe. 'Or else Julie was just trying to scare us off — it would be like her not to shoot, when she'll guess we won't shoot back because she's a woman!'

The car was racing up the increasing incline at top speed still, though in another few hundred yards the steepness of the climb caused Lowe to slam through into second gear.

He had already realised, to his chagrin, that the car ahead was, if anything, a trifle faster than their own. The distance between the two cars had been increased. But their second gear seemed higher than that of the car in front, and now, thanks to the uphill going, they were beginning to diminish the distance between pursued and pursuers.

Where Julie was making for was a problem that Lowe would have given a good deal to have been able to answer. So far the girl spy was keeping to the coast road, driving as if with set purpose, when they might have expected her to turn aside and plunge into the maze of twisting minor roads among the hills, as more likely to give her a chance to throw her pursuers off her track.

'She's got some scheme in her head, I'll be bound!' muttered Dene. 'Jove — we're over-hauling 'em — '

There was no more than a couple of hundred yards between the two cars now.

Both were still tearing up the long incline in second gear. But in another minute the leading machine had gained the crest of the hill. It vanished over the top.

'And they're faster on the level!' rasped Lowe with set face. 'But we'll overhaul 'em yet!'

They roared over the crest of the hill.

The beating wind met them, whistling past them shrilly, and a sweeping panorama of cliffs and moonlit sea. Away over the hills to their left, a pale gleam of dawn was showing like a grey smear. Ahead, along the snaking, undulating road, the car that contained Julie and Leon, the Frenchman, was racing away, well ahead once more. Lowe slipped the gear lever into top, and they tore in pursuit.

At any cost, Julie had to be robbed of her precious prize — the stolen treaty draft that meant so much to the British Foreign Office — and Lowe was not troubling about risks.

314

The long, level stretch had given their quarry a chance to draw farther ahead yet. But another uphill stretch that called for second gear gave the pursuers the opportunity to lessen the intervening distance once more.

'A long hill, and we've got 'em!' jerked out Lowe. 'And there it is!'

They were tearing down a long slope into a shallow dip among the cliffs, the red light of the leading car racing ahead of them nearly a quarter of a mile away. But beyond, on the far side of the dip, a long, dark hillside, with the road snaking up it in a mile-long climb, had loomed; a wild, lonely road, with hairpin bends hanging high over sheer rocky slopes, and beetling rocks towering at places on either side, narrowing the road dangerously.

'I'll back this car to overtake 'em before they get to the top of that!'

Lowe's voice was quiet. But White, behind him, recognised the relentless note that he knew so well.

Their headlamps splashing white through the gloom, as a dark cloud wiped out the moon, they flew down the hill and took the opposite slope. Already the lights of the French girl's car were racing up the dark hillside. They saw it swing round the curve, its bend by the cliff edge, and Dene caught his breath. It seemed to him that the leading car had almost met disaster.

'That girl can drive!' muttered Dene admiringly.

His face was set as he peered through the windscreen up the wild hillside, watching the racing headlamps of the car above them as it climbed higher, taking the dangerous bends at almost suicidal speed, as their own car roared in pursuit.

That they were gaining on their quarry was clear enough.

'We've got 'em!' ejaculated Arnold tensely. 'If they don't crash — '

The words snapped off.

The leading car, plainly visible on one of the upper stretches of the snaking, uphill road, had reached another of the wind-swept zig-zag bends that until then Julie had negotiated with such superb skill and reckless daring. They saw it swing round the corner, its headlamps white on the stony road — saw the red rear-light sway outwards towards the edge, where the cliffs dropped steeply from the low stone wall that guarded the bend.

'She's skidded — '

The hoarse cry came from Dene.

Mademoiselle Julie, risking all in her desperate attempt to beat her pursuers, and win for her country the precious documents that she had fought for with such reckless daring, had taken one risk too many.

The loose, treacherous road-surface had betrayed her. Those in the pursuing car saw the skidding vehicle crash through the low stone wall at the edge of the twisting road, swing out over the drop, and come to rest with its rear wheels in mid-air, the broken wall piled beneath the under-carriage holding it half on the road, half out over the sheer brink.

At any moment, it was clear, the machine might slip backwards and crash to destruction on the rocky cliffside beneath. There was horror in their faces and they knew that the life of Mlle. Julie hung at that moment on a thread.

Then a shadowy figure appeared, climbing swiftly from the overhanging car, clutching at the broken wall, dragging itself to safety. Dene drew a long, whistling breath between his teeth.

A second figure followed — Leon, the Frenchman. The two figures stood for a moment staring down at the swiftly climbing car below them, then vanished abruptly into the shadows.

The wrecked car was still hanging with its rear wheels over the cliff-side as Lowe drew his own car to a standstill within a few yards of it, and the three leapt out.

There was no sign of Julie and her companion. The rocky hillside offered innumerable opportunities for cover.

'They're not giving in!' said Lowe. 'Hope to give us the slip yet. But they can't be far away.'

As he spoke a loose stone, rattling down on to the road almost at their feet from somewhere above, cut his words short.

'There they go!'

He had glimpsed a shadowy shape slipping from one of the rocks on the hillside above into the cover of another.

He sprang for the steep bank at the edge of the road, scrambling upwards up the steep boulder-strewn slope. Dene followed with White.

For a moment a break in the clouds revealed the moon, and the white light flooded the wild hillside. They caught sight of two figures outlined for a moment against the sky as they scrambled round a jutting shoulder of cliff. The next moment a bullet came singing down above their heads.

'Another little warning' rasped Dene. 'Leon!'

They did not pause in their swift upward scramble. They gained the shoulder of cliff over which their quarry had vanished, and found that beyond it another rock-strewn slope dropped away towards the cliff-edge. No sign now of Julie and the Frenchman.

'This is a blindfold game!' growled Dene, lying between two shadowy boulders and peering keenly down the slope. 'Julie'll stick at nothing to get away with the goods! She'll keep shooting all right, even though I don't suppose she'll shoot to kill. Keep down — '

Even as he spoke, Arnold, who had raised his head, ducked with an ejaculation, as another bullet came whining at them, from somewhere on the slope below. It struck the rocks to their left, and the splinters flew.

'If I can put a bullet in Leon's leg I'll be glad to do it!' grunted Dene.

One of the flying rock-splinters had gashed his cheek, and the fingers he raised to his face came away darkly wet.

Crouching behind the little group of rocks the three of them peered cautiously ahead. To have ventured over that shoulder of hill, outlined as they would have been against the moonlit sky, would have been useless. They would have provided a target that no one could miss. And that Leon was lying somewhere among the opposite rocks, covering the retreat of Mademoiselle Julie, was certain enough.

'That's their scheme, for sure,' muttered Lowe. 'Leon holding us here while the girl gets away with the treaty! Curse this moonlight!'

He was staring up at the sky. The heavy clouds were again drifting around the moon. It would not be long before the moonlight was once more blotted out, when they could take the risk of leaving cover. But the delay was maddening, knowing as they did that every minute was doubtless putting Julie farther from them, safer from their pursuit.

The clouds closed over the moon abruptly. In a moment the three of them had risen to their feet, were racing down the slope. A bullet sang between them, and they saw the stab of flame from the Frenchman's weapon, away to their left. Dene whipped up his gun and sent an answering shot whining towards the spot from which that pencil of flame had come. He had no fear of hitting Julie; Julie, they were reasonably sure, was already well away from the spot while her companion covered her retreat.

Again the Frenchman fired. The bullet tore through Lowe's sleeve, from barely a dozen yards away.

The dramatist hurled himself through the gloom towards the group of dim-seen rocks. A figure rose in the shadows with an upraised weapon in its hand, and Lowe saw the glimmer in the French-man's eyes. Then the two men were at grips. Lowe's left hand clutched like steel round Leon's wrist, twisting the hot weapon from the man's fingers. It fell among the boulders among which they were struggling in a fierce embrace, and then Dene, stumbling over the boulders, rammed the nose of his automatic into the Frenchman's back.

'I'd be a good boy if I were you, Leon!' he rasped softly. 'I'd hate to have to hurt a pal of Julie's.'

The Frenchman froze, rigid, at the touch of the weapon that was nosing up against his spine. Slowly he raised his arms, his face malevolent. Lowe stepped back.

'Where's mademoiselle?' he jerked out.

The Frenchman shrugged, but did not answer

Swiftly Lowe ran his hands over the man's pockets. He had no hope that the stolen treaty was on the Frenchman — that was in Julie's possession, for certain. But there might be something in Leon's pockets of value to them — something to indicate where Julie was likely to make for, if she eluded them now on the cliffs.

His search, however, was unrewarded. There was a harsh laugh from Leon.

'Well, mes amis?' he asked derisively. 'What now, messieurs? I am your prisoner!'

'Tie his hands, White!' rasped Lowe. 'And look after him. We'll trail Julie yet!'

'I think you are too late,' murmured Leon mockingly, as he stood unresisting, while Arnold lashed his wrists.

'Too late. What do you mean?' jerked out Dene, swiftly.

It had struck him that there was some secret significance in the Frenchman's words.

Leon shrugged smilingly, and remained silent.

Again the moon had broken abruptly through the clouds. Lowe gave a sudden exclamation.

'Look at that!'

A dark spot on one of the rocks by their

feet had caught his eye. It was a smear of blood.

The Frenchman bore no sign of any wound. It was clearly Julie who had left that spot of blood, and Lowe guessed that the girl-spy had torn her hand in dragging herself to safety from the wrecked car. From the size of the smear it was evident that the girl's hand was bleeding fairly profusely.

He dragged a torch from his pocket, and the beam of torchlight swept round over the moonlit rocks. Among the shadows beneath them the white ray revealed another spot of blood — and another.

'This is the way she went!'

Leon's face had changed. But Lowe was not looking at the Frenchman. Scrambling over the boulders, the detective was already following the trail of fallen blood. Dene followed him, leaving Arnold, gun in hand, seated on a boulder watching his prisoner.

Once or twice they had difficulty in following the spots of blood on the stones and on the windswept grass. But each time they picked up the trail again and followed it. It led them down towards the cliff-edge, to a point where a narrow cliff path vanished over the brink, evidently leading to the shore.

The sea-wind blustering round them, they climbed down the tortuous path in single file. The drops of blood were infrequent now, then stopped altogether. It looked as though the French girl had paused at that point to bind up her wounded hand. But the path they were following could only lead to one place — the cove beneath.

'What the deuce has brought her down here?' muttered Lowe, in bewilderment, as they reached the shingle at last, and stood peering round. 'What's her scheme?'

The cove was steeped in darkness, the high flanking cliffs shutting out the moon-light utterly. Beyond the shingle, the waves were beating in noisily, the opening sea behind silver in the light of the moon.

'She's not here!'

Dark though it was in the little cove, their eyes were used to the gloom, and the sheer walls of cliff gave no opportunity for cover. Dene flung out a pointing hand.

'Must have gone that way!'

He was pointing towards the rocks at the base of the headland on their left. Dangerous though the climb would be, it looked as though by means of it the next cover could be reached. There seemed no other way by which Julie could have gone; and a minute later they were scrambling over the slimy rocks, making their hazardous way round the base of the blunt headland. A wide stretch of shadowy shingle lay beyond the headland, between two more jutting arms of cliff. As they gained it, there was a sudden ejaculation from Lowe.

'Look!'

Drawn up at the edge of the water near the base of the opposite headland, revealed clear in the moonlight, was a long, lean motor-boat.

In a flash, Lowe understood.

Julie had had this motor-boat waiting in readiness all along; it was for that reason that she had chosen the cliff-road in her flight that night. And she had almost reached the spot for which she had been making, when disaster had overcome her speeding car, almost putting her into her pursuers' hands.

Her plan was to elude further pursuit by escaping by water. And it was only the state of the tide, as Lowe realised, that had prevented the French girl from getting clear away, minutes before.

They could see her standing by the launch, staring back anxiously — already she had seen them. But as yet, it seemed, the rising tide had not floated the waiting launch, and the girl alone had not strength to thrust the heavy craft out into the waves.

'I fancy Julie is caught at last!' said Lowe quietly. 'That treaty won't be travelling to France after all!'

A long stretch of beach separated them from the girl by the launch at the water's edge. And now, as they moved quickly towards her, they saw her raise her hand.

The crack of Julie's automatic echoed against the wall of cliff behind her, as the bullet passed above their heads. They broke into a run, their feet slipping loosely in the piled shingle. Again Julie fired; and this time it was clear that she was firing to hit. The whining lead flew close by Lowe's feet.

But they kept on. There was no cover; and already they had both seen that the swiftly rising tide, washing round the launch, might at any moment lift it from the shingle, and give the French girl her way of escape. Pounding grimly over the loose stones that impeded their every stride, they kept on.

A third bullet, splashing the shingle close behind Dene's feet. Then a fourth, that tore through the flesh of his right forearm.

'Come on!' cried Lowe. 'Look — that launch is floating!'

An extra large wave had rolled in under the hull of the launch, lifting it buoyantly, dragging it down the steep sloping shingle. It came to rest again — then another wave took it, floated it high, as Julie leapt for the sliding bows.

They raced forward desperately. But the loose shingle prevented the necessary turn of speed; they heard the launch's engines roar noisily, saw the lean shape sliding out from the shore stern-first with increasing speed as the screw threshed the water. A curling wave smashed over the stern, the spray flinging past the slender, graceful figure that stood at the tiller, as Julie waved her hand with gay mockery to the two running figures on the beach. Across the widening strip of intervening water, they heard her clear voice, her rippling laugh:

'Farewell, mes amis! Au revoir! I win — n'est ce pas?'

The launch was turning, fifty yards out from shore. Its swaying bows headed for the open sea, it began to slide rapidly through the waves, with ever-increasing speed.

Lowe's face was set in hard lines.

'She's a woman, Dene! But she's got our country's secrets — '

He half-raised his automatic, then lowered it again. Side by side, the two men stood watching as the launch vanished round the headland, the slim, girlish figure in the stern still standing poised by the tiller — vanished with a last mocking wave of her hand, a derisively blown kiss.

'Dene, she can be stopped yet — stopped from getting to France! We must find a wireless station — get in touch with the Admiralty, have orders sent out to all men-of-war — '

'I don't feel inclined to have Julie stopped, even if she could be,' broke in Dene coolly. 'She's a rare little sports-woman, Lowe. And after all, she saved our lives tonight, when Ni was going to swing us, on board the *Oki Maru*!'

'But the treaty, man!' jerked out Lowe impatiently.

Dene's queer, glimmering blue eyes fastened on his with a grim smile.

'Hang it, you wouldn't begrudge Julie her win, would you, after she saved our necks?' he demanded.

Lowe stared at him in astonishment.

'You don't mean to say you can feel satisfied?'

Dene nodded.

'I am perfectly satisfied,' he said gruffly.

Again the queer smile touched his lips.

'You see, I have rather a tender spot in my heart for Julie,' he explained. 'Friend or foe, I can't help that! I don't begrudge her her hour of triumph a moment, Lowe, honestly.'

He winced as he stirred his wounded arm.

'You see,' he went on softly, 'her hour of triumph, I am afraid, won't last very long! Not when she examines those papers she's got!'

'What the deuce do you mean?' breathed Lowe.

For something in the voice of the other had told him that Dene was hugging some intense inward amusement.

'It was a mean trick on my part, not telling you the truth before!' chuckled Dene. 'But I just couldn't resist it!'

'For heaven's sake, explain!' muttered Lowe. 'What do you mean?'

'Julie bought a pup!' grinned Dene abruptly. 'That's what I mean! Did you think I would really have handed the treaty over to Ni so easily? I could at least have heaved it into the water, where the sea-water would have made most of it undecipherable before they could manage to find and recover it! Lord, no! While I was arguing the toss with Ni — sailing for time, of course — I had my hand in my pocket. Notice that?'

331

He chuckled deeply.

'I had my notes and report of the case for the Foreign Office in there, too,' drawled the Secret Service man. 'I had written 'em up this morning, to send to Whitehall. I managed to attach the top sheet of the treaty to my own report — and it was that I handed to Ni! He didn't examine any more than the top sheet, and neither did Julie. The Foreign Office stamp was good enough for them! And, of course, it was the top sheet of the treaty, anyhow — though that won't tell them anything, being the usual preamble of introduction to these things.'

Again he paused to chuckle heartily.

'Well, my notes and report won't tell them any secrets other than perhaps a code word or two — and I'll tell 'em in the Department to have those altered! Poor Julie — I'm sorry for her! I'm afraid she won't be pleased when she finds out!'

Lowe drew a deep breath.

'By Jove, Dene — so we win, after all!'

'You bet we win!' growled Michael Dene, with a crooked smile. 'And in the circumstances we can afford to let Leon go.'

★ ★ ★

Dawn had broken when Inspector Williams, who had been back at the house from Caermawr for some little time, wondering what had happened to Lowe and Dene, arrived in the cavern with three uniformed constables.

And in another fifteen minutes Tsu Ni, wounded but conscious once more, with a pair of handcuffs glittering on his fleshy wrists, was being ushered into the big old house, his eyes diabolical, for he knew that he was not only beaten, but would soon be facing the consequences of his crimes.

The other man who still lived, one of the white men from the *Sea Witch*, was with his master, also handcuffed. But for the while the man who was dead still lay on the rusted deck of the *Oki Maru*, in the shadows and the silence.

Puhm, the murderer of K'Yung, the second mate of the ill-fated Japanese steamer, would never now face the hangman for that crime, nor for the murder of Police-sergeant Owen in the grounds of the old house high above his head.

But the murderer of Sir Matthew Moncrieff, the spy from the *Sea Witch*, whom Ni had sent to the house on that night when Lowe and White had come to the old mansion on the Welsh cliffs, and there had found Michael Dene — that murderer was not, like Puhm, to escape his period of waiting in a condemned cell. For the fugitive ruffians from the cavern were traced and captured a few miles from Caermawr, and Lowe in due course proved that the cat-like little Korean among them had been the murderer of Moncrieff.

It was about three days later that a letter arrived for Michael Dene at the Foreign Office, bearing a French stamp and a Paris post-mark.

He recognised the writing on the envelope, and he ripped the envelope open, with a rugged smile. He glanced through the contents, and his smile broadened, before he handed the letter across to Lowe, who had looked in to see him that afternoon, and was sitting in Dene's most comfortable chair.

He took the letter inquiringly, then he, too, smiled and chuckled.

'Moncher Monsieur,' the letter ran. 'You are the clever man, you know! I am, oh, so angry with you! But I can admire, too. Next time, perhaps, I shall beat you. But that we shall see, n'est ce pas? But this time you must accept my sincere congratulations, monsieur, for your so clever wits! Yes, you win!'

The signature was a single initial: 'J.'
'She's a sportswoman is Julie!' murmured Lowe as he handed the letter back to his friend. 'Only a sportswoman would have written to tell us so!'
'She is!' nodded Michael Dene softly.

THE END

We do hope that you have enjoyed reading this large print book.

Did you know that all of our titles are available for purchase?

We publish a wide range of high quality large print books including:
Romances, Mysteries, Classics
General Fiction
Non Fiction and Westerns

Special interest titles available in large print are:
The Little Oxford Dictionary
Music Book, Song Book
Hymn Book, Service Book

Also available from us courtesy of Oxford University Press:
Young Readers' Dictionary
(large print edition)
Young Readers' Thesaurus
(large print edition)

For further information or a free brochure, please contact us at:
Ulverscroft Large Print Books Ltd.,
The Green, Bradgate Road, Anstey,
Leicester, LE7 7FU, England.
Tel: (00 44) **0116 236 4325**
Fax: (00 44) **0116 234 0205**

Other titles in the
Linford Mystery Library:

DEATH ASKS THE QUESTIONS

John Russell Fearn

Seemingly grand from the outside, the interior of Abner Hilton's house was a dilapidated, gloomy place — reflecting its morbid and desperately impoverished occupant. But Hilton's insane plan would lift him out of his poverty. He would murder his young niece, who was about to visit him; her dead father's will would ensure that her considerable wealth would pass to him. However, when his plan was put into operation, the young woman's horrifying death was to have terrifying repercussions . . .

ENTER JIMMY STRANGE

Ernest Dudley

'What type of skulduggery is the Master Mind contemplating this time?' That was the question put to Jimmy Strange by his long-suffering girlfriend Sandra. But the answer always depended on which type of criminals Jimmy was pitting his wits against. Whether they were poisoners, gunmen, murderers, drug dealers, or jewel thieves, they were all operating, untouched, outside the law — until Jimmy entered the scene — and he was not averse to using their own methods against them . . .